THE BARON'S MALADY

A SMITHFIELD MARKET REGENCY ROMANCE
(BOOK 4)

ROSE PEARSON

LANDON HILL MEDIA

© Copyright 2018 by Rose Pearson - All rights reserved.

In no way is it legal to reproduce, duplicate, or transmit any part of this document by either electronic means or in printed format. Recording of this publication is strictly prohibited and any storage of this document is not allowed unless with written permission from the publisher. All rights reserved.

Respective author owns all copyrights not held by the publisher.

❦ Created with Vellum

THE BARON'S MALADY

CHAPTER ONE

Miss Josephine Noe, daughter to the late deceased Mr. and Mrs. Noe, sat quietly on a grubby step in Smithfield Market, trying her best to stop the cold wind from getting in through her moth-eaten shawl. Her unshod feet were raw with cold and she attempted to tuck them under her grubby skirts. Her eyes were red but there were no more tears left. She had nothing left within her to give. All she had to do now was survive.

The wind whipped about her and she shivered, trying her best to ignore the grumbling of her stomach. It had been hours since she'd last eaten and, even then, it had only been a half-rotten apple and a moldy bit of bread she'd found in an alleyway. There was nothing going spare and since she was only one of hundreds of beggars on the street, it wasn't likely she'd be able to survive if things carried on this way.

She'd thought to come to London from her home in

Hampstead, hoping that she'd somehow find work and be able to scratch out a living, but that dream had died almost the moment she'd set foot in the city. There was nothing here but disease and death. The very same disease that had taken her parents and forced her from her village.

When her parents had become ill, she'd done everything she could to help them, but to no avail. What had made things all the worse was that she too had become sick but, for whatever reason, had managed to recover from it. She could still remember the ache in her throat, her pounding head, and skin that itched and burned. Her days had been filled with delirium until, finally, she'd emerged weak and frail, but no longer ill.

It had not been that way for her parents. Unable to do anything to help them, she had seen them taken from her one after the other. The agony of that still tore at her, bringing tears to her eyes whenever she so much as thought of it.

The village had not wanted her to linger, however. They had heard of this disease sweeping through nearby towns and had demanded that she leave the village for good, even though she had already had the disease and then recovered. There had been no other choice for her and she'd realized that it was fear that had forced her friends and neighbors to act as they did. Doing as they'd asked without protest, she'd taken the few things she had left and walked away from the only place she'd called home. The village folk had burned her parent's cottage to the ground, doing all they could to prevent the disease from spreading.

Josephine prayed that the village folk were safe. She was not angry with them for treating her as though she were some kind of leper, remembering how mothers had clutched their children to them as she had passed. Being in London these last weeks, she had seen just how truly awful this 'scarlet fever' was. The disease was terrifying in its swiftness, taking men, women, and children – although the children and the weak were often the ones doomed for death. Her heart twisted with pain and she rested her head on her knees for a moment. What was she to do now? Was she truly to have escaped death in Hampstead, only to face it again in London? If she did not eat, then she would soon be too weak to move and would end up being just another urchin dead on the streets of London.

Her body shuddered with the cold as the wind pierced her thin cotton dress, trying to make its way into her very soul. Hope was gone from her. She had nothing left in this world, nothing she could call her own. There was no-one to turn to, no-one whom she could go to for aid. Winter was coming and Josephine did not know what she was to do.

"Buy your bread 'ere!"

Her head shot up, hope running through her. The bread cart was passing by. People began to flock to it and, as Josephine watched, she saw a young beggar boy nip up to the cart. He was gone in a moment, a loaf of bread held tightly in his hand, his face lit up with a grin.

Josephine caught her breath. She did not want to steal, knowing that everyone was just trying to make a living of their own, but if she did not have something to eat then she would not last. She had to take what she could from where she could.

A shudder ran through her. The last time she had tried to take something from one of the market street sellers on Smithfield Market, she had almost been caught. Her hand had curled around an apple and thrust it into the pocket of her dress, just as a ruckus had started up only a few feet away from her. She could still remember the sight of it. A young boy, grubby, dirty and afraid, was screaming for his life. In his hand, he clasped something shiny, which she had known at once to be a coin. He'd obviously stolen it from someone and been caught and the terror in his face had burned into her soul. She could still remember how she'd backed away, her eyes fixed on the boy as a grown man had held him tightly. The constabulary had arrived, shouting loudly as they'd pushed their way through the crowd.

And then, the man holding the child had let out a scream of pain, taking his hand from the child as he twisted away. The boy had bitten him – a desperate act in order to get away. The constables had run immediately after him, their shouts of rage seeming to echo straight through her.

"Mark my words," she'd heard someone say. "It'll be the gaol for that young lad, if they catch him. He won't ever see the light of day again, I reckon."

"Let's hope they don't catch him then," said another man, with a wry smile on his face. "Poor beggar."

"Careful there!"

The shout brought Josephine back to the present, back to her grumbling stomach and the ever-present fear of being caught. She could not be sent to gaol. The very thought sent terror straight through her, her heart quickening its pace at the fear of being thrown into some dark and dingy cell, with only rats for company. *He won't ever see the light of day again.*

Those words had her fixed to her step, despite the desperate urge to eat.

The man pulling the bread roll cart began to wave his arms as the people jostled about. A bread roll fell from the cart, landing on the cobbled street as the cart moved away.

Immediately, Josephine's eyes fixed on it. For a moment, her fear and her hunger battled against one another until, finally, she moved without hesitation. Dodging in between men and women, some with baskets and some who glared at her as though she were an annoying fly buzzing about their presence, she kept her gaze fixed on the small, dirty bread roll.

Her hands clasped about it with such gratitude that she almost felt like crying, but she knew she could not eat it here. Running back to where she had come from, she quickly sat down to eat, her teeth tearing off large chunks of bread as she grew desperate to satisfy the growl of her stomach.

Tears ran down her cheeks as she ate. This was not the life she was used to. Her father had been a laborer and her mother had taken in all manner of work in order to bring in a little extra money. She had helped her mother with the sewing and darning, with the herbs and remedies her mother had put together to help those who were sick, and what had been all the more wonderful was when she had been offered the chance to work as a maid at one of the great houses in Hampstead. It had brought a good wage with it, although she had been forced to improve herself in a good many ways even though she barely interacted with those in the house. The housekeeper had taken great pains to improve her speech, her posture, her manner of walking and her appearance. It had been difficult to be apart from her parents but it had been the chance to have a different life and, until the day she got word that her parents had become ill, she had enjoyed it. It was not a rich or abundant life, of course, but it was still a life where she had plenty to appreciate and enjoy. The money she had made working as a maid had been sent back to her parents for the most part, making sure that they never had to scrape about for food. They had never once had to consider stealing simply to satisfy their hunger. There had never been a lot, but there had always been enough. Now, even though she was alone on the London streets, she hated the thought of stealing but knew she would have to do so in order to survive.

She wiped away the tears with the back of her hand, leaving a grimy smudge on her cheek. Her fingers were red with cold but at least the roll brought a little contentment – not that it would last long. Closing her eyes, Josephine tried not to let doubts fill her. She had come to London in the hope of becoming a maid in one of the grand houses, but no-one would so much as look at her, not when she had nothing but the clothes on her back and no references of any sort. She would have had references, of course, had she not had to leave her position in the great house with barely a day's notice. But she had not been able to stay away, knowing that her parents needed her. So now, what was she to do? Was she to simply beg on the streets and pray to God that she would somehow make it through the winter? Was there nothing she could do?

"You there!"

Her breath caught and she forced herself to remain entirely still, frozen in place on her step.

"You! Girl!"

Slowly lifting her head, Josephine saw a tall, dark-haired gentleman moving towards her. He was wearing fine clothes, walking with the dignity and air of a gentleman. There was strength in his movement and, as he approached her, Josephine saw the slight lift of his chin and wrinkling of his nose, which betrayed his disinclination for the area surrounding Smithfield Market.

"Y-yes, my lord?" she stammered, wondering if she ought to stand but being a little unsure as to whether or not her legs would hold her up. "Can I help you?"

"Yes." He tossed her a coin which clattered to the ground. Josephine stared at it for a moment, before picking it up with cold fingers. She held it tightly in her palm, hardly daring to believe she had been given something so precious.

"Do you know your way about this place?"

Carefully, she got to her feet. "I do, my lord," she replied, hope bursting in her heart.

"I need to find a particular address and appear to

have become rather lost. I thought to walk, you see, since the day was fine," the gentleman replied, looking at her steadily. "You appear to be in need of some assistance also. If you are able to deliver me to where I need to go, then I shall be glad to recompense you in some way."

Josephine swallowed hard and nodded, the coin clutched tightly in her hand. He was to give her more, perhaps? More money meant that she would not have to struggle for food for some days, for the coin she had meant food for at least a week!

"I should be glad to help you, my lord," she replied, carefully, letting her gaze travel to his face and finding that there was now a small smile on his handsome face. In fact, he appeared to be quite at his ease and she found herself smiling back.

"Very good," he responded, grandly. "I am Baron Dunstable. I am charged with calling upon a family friend to take them to my estate for a prolonged visit." His expression changed. "The disease is taking hold of London and I must get her safe." Josephine noticed that his gaze had drifted away by this point and it was as if he were speaking to himself. She hesitated, waiting for him to say more, only for him to clear his throat and turn his attention back to her. Frowning, his brows burrowed down as he looked at her carefully. "You are not unwell, I hope?"

"Oh, no, my lord," Josephine replied, hastily. "That is, I have already had the fever and it has gone from me."

His expression cleared. "I see. You have recovered then?"

"Yes, my lord. A few weeks ago it was now."

Nodding slowly, the gentleman studied her for another moment or two. "You speak very well for a...." He trailed off, clearly unwilling to call her what she was – a street urchin. She managed a small smile, hating her wretched appearance.

"I was a maid in a great house in Hampstead for a time," she said, by way of explanation. "The housekeeper there spent a lot of time working with me."

The explanation seemed to satisfy him. "I see," he murmured, his gaze a little interested. Stretching out his arm towards the pavement, his lips curved upwards into a small smile. "Then might we go, miss?"

A faint heat crept into her cheeks, embarrassed. "My lord, you have not said where you wish to go." She dropped her head only to hear him chuckle with exasperation.

"Indeed, I have not. It is not too far, I think." Quickly, he gave her the address and Josephine, relieved that she knew precisely where to go, began to hurry through the streets of Smithfield Market.

As they walked in silence, Josephine felt her despair begin to fall away. She would not have to worry about food or shelter for a time, if the gentleman was to be as generous as he promised. His funds would not give her any permanent solution, of course, not unless his fiancée's household was looking for a chamber maid, but at least it would take the fear from her back for a time.

"Have you no work?"

She turned her head, a little astonished that the gentleman would consider speaking to someone as lowly as she. "I – I cannot find any, my lord," she stammered, feeling heat rise in her face as she tried her best to speak properly. "I came from Hampstead to find work here but none would take me."

"From Hampstead, you say," he replied, easily, as they walked past the Smithfield House for Girls. "Why did you come to London? Was there no work for you back home?"

"The fever took my parents." The words came from her lips with no emotion attached to them, although it tore her apart inwardly. So many had lost loved ones, so many felt the same pain and grief she endured. She was just another one left alone on the earth, lost, afraid and without hope. Silently, she wondered if the Baron, being of the nobility, had lost any of his dear ones to the fever. Surely not, given just how different his circumstances were from her own!

"I am very sorry to hear of your loss, miss," he murmured, as they turned the corner into another street. "That must have been very painful for you."

She nodded but said nothing. She could not. The ache in her chest was becoming too great.

"My father recently passed away," he continued, as though he were simply talking to a friend. "That is why I am to return to his estate, although I suppose it is to be my estate now." Sighing heavily, he came to stand beside her as she came to a stop at the end of the designated street. "Grief affects all of us, does it not? No matter our circumstances."

Josephine felt herself wondering about this gentleman. He appeared both kind and gracious, which was not what she had come to expect from those in the nobility.

Most often, they simply rode or walked past people like her, ignoring them completely, whereas Baron Dunstable seemed to be rather interested in her.

"You must be careful," he was saying, as she gestured towards the house where his fiancée would be waiting for him. "A young lady like yourself could easily become the prey of those who have less than pleasant intentions."

She managed a small smile, aware of just how intense his blue eyes were when they lingered on her. A little ashamed of her ragged dress and grimy face, she dropped her gaze and nodded. "Thank you, my lord. You are most kind."

The gentleman smiled at her again, his eyes alight. "Very good, miss. Now here, take this and ensure that you spend it wisely." He placed some coins in her palm but she did not look at them, barely able to keep her breathing steady. This was more than she had ever dared hope for.

"I think you will be wise with them, however," he continued, with a broad smile. "Thank you for your excellent navigation through the streets of London. I am in your debt." He bowed towards her, as though she were some elegant lady, before turning on his heel and walking away.

Josephine remained precisely where she was for a good few minutes, watching him as he left. Her breathing was quickening as she felt the coins in her hand, her legs shaking just a little as she slowly unwrapped her fingers to look down at them.

She gasped. The gentleman had given her five sovereigns. Five full sovereigns. That was more than her parents had earned in a year! Her eyes filled with tears and she held her hand close to her chest, feeling the warm tears slip down her cheeks. There was more than just money here, there was a place to sleep, food to eat, warm tea to drink and revive her. It would give her the chance to find work without fearing where her next meal would come from. Baron Dunstable had not simply given her money, he had given her a life. She would not need to fear the winter, nor even the one after that if she was careful.

Pulling her ragged handkerchief from her pocket, she wrapped up the coins tightly and tied a knot, making sure they would not jingle for fear they might be stolen. "Bless you," she whispered, watching him through tear filled eyes. "Bless you, good sir. And thank you."

CHAPTER TWO

"Georgina, really. You need not fuss!"

Miss Georgina Wells, daughter to Viscount Armitage, frowned heavily at Gideon and continued to smooth and rearrange her skirts.

"Georgina, please," he said again, growing frustrated with her constant attempts to ensure her skirts had not a single wrinkle in them. "You will only have to do so again once we reach the estate, which will be very soon."

"Then it is all the more important that I am quite ready and prepared to meet your mother and dear sister again, is it not?" Georgina replied, primly. "Really, Dunstable, you are quite impossible sometimes! Can you not see that this is of the utmost importance, especially since it is my new gown?"

Gideon held his tongue with an effort, despite the fact that he wanted nothing more than to state there was nothing wrong with Georgina's skirts and that no, new dresses were not of the utmost importance. Looking out of the window at the familiar landscape, he tried to let the frustration pass from him. He had known Georgina for a good many years and had always known that she did not care for anything other than herself. It was to be expected, of course, given that she was a young lady of quality who had been brought up to preen and simper and delight in everything she did and everywhere she went – but of late, it was beginning to grate on him. Mayhap it was because he had finally realized that the death of his father meant that he now had sole charge of the estate and all that went with it. Mayhap it was because there was this terrible fever sweeping through London, taking so many to the grave with it. For whatever reason, Gideon found himself growing more and more irritated with his bride to be. He did not care about new gowns or the like and was surprised that Georgina appeared to put so much stock into what she wore or whether or not the gown was of the highest fashion. Did she not see all that was going on around her? Did she not see the sick, the fallen, the poor and the needy? It was all he had been aware of since coming to London some days ago.

Sighing to himself, Gideon fixed his gaze on the window and did not let himself listen to Georgina's continued complaints about his lack of consideration for her and her gown. They had been betrothed for a good many years, due to the desire of both Gideon's father and Georgina's father, but he had never felt anything particularly for her and, even though he had not asked her, Gideon did not think that Georgina had any particular affection for him. That being said, whilst he had never found her particularly engaging, she certainly was beautiful and did well to be every bit the elegant lady she was expected to be – although Gideon was quite sure she had not been this vapid when he had first left for India two years ago, at the behest of his father. Having holdings in India, Gideon's father had thought it would be good for his son to see for himself what things were like and Gideon had rather enjoyed his time there, managing and ordering things. To hear that his father was deathly ill, however, had brought his joy to an end and so he had taken the first passage he could back home. It had been too late, however, for he had missed the funeral itself by over a month. Now that their half mourning was completed, Gideon was finally able to step back into society just a little, which meant that Georgina could make a long-planned visit to the estate.

Except, he did not feel any particular joy at the prospect.

His mind drifted back to the young lady he had seen on the steps, the one who had helped him to find his way. He could still recall how she had looked up at him with wide green eyes, clearly astonished that he would stop to talk to her. At one point, she had moved back from him, as though fearing he would either strike her or drag her away and he had felt his heart break. There were so many beggar children, so many orphans and street urchins but there had been something about this young lady that had spoken to his heart. Whether or not it was because he was afraid that she might be taken advantage of, beaten or worse, he had given her more than he had intended in the hope that she would make as much use of it as she could.

He had not meant to become lost in Smithfield Market, of course. He had been in the center of London and had become more and more astonished at just how desolate it seemed to be. It had not been the London he remembered, for it was quiet with an almost oppressive air. There had not been hackneys ready to take him to wherever he needed to go. There had not been carriages filled with the *ton*, all laughing and smiling and desperate to be seen. The quietness of it had been all the more evidenced by the fact that this was only just the end of the Season, a time when there ought to be at least a few more balls and soirees – but there had been nothing of the sort. The fever had scared the wealthy away, back to their country estates where they prayed they would be safe.

That fear had begun to linger in his own heart. His feet had ached in his boots as he had turned this way and that, growing a little more desperate with every minute that had passed. Having thought to go to the townhouse of his fiancée's father, he had begun to pray that he would either find his way there or somehow manage to make his way back to his own townhouse but had not managed to do either. It was obvious that Smithfield Market was no place for a gentleman of the *ton*. Men and women had jostled him without any consideration, shooting either vengeful glances or interested, conniving looks as if wondering what they could take from him. If he were to be attacked, he had realized, there would be no-one to come to his aid. The air had grown thick and his heart had quickened with anxiety. Despite this, however, he had lifted his head high and continued on as best he could, all too aware that the streets of Smithfield Market were not exactly safe.

The fever was in Smithfield Market too, he was well aware of that. As he had walked, a woman near him had stopped to cough violently, which had forced a frisson of fear into his heart.

Seeing the young lady sitting on that step had jolted that fear from his bones. She did not look as though she were about to attack him or steal from him, for he could sense a desperation coming from her. Her eyes were red-rimmed as if she had been crying, her feet bare and hands red with cold - and his compassion for her had burst to life. It was clear that she was living from one day to the next, never quite sure where her food would come from – and so he had taken a chance. A chance that had paid off for them both.

The grime on her forehead, the way her dark hair had swept about her thin cheekbones – he could not forget her face. How different she was to Georgina, and yet how much more in need of his assistance than his fiancée. Georgina came from wealth. He had more than enough to live on quite comfortably and yet that young lady, who he was sure was almost the same age as Georgina, had nothing. Her parents were gone and she had no work to speak of. Even though she spoke well and clearly had been given a very basic education from the housekeeper where she had worked, the young lady had no employment. None would hire her, he was sure, not if they discovered that she had already had the fever. Everyone was afraid, even of someone who had been struck with it, only to survive. He had spoken to her more than he had first intended, finding his heart caught with sympathy for her and aware of just how grateful she had been to him for what, for him, was a simple kindness. He prayed that she would not fritter away the coins he had given her, but that she would use it to find food and shelter for herself. He had wanted to do more, had wanted to demand that Georgina ensure the girl had a position as a maid or some such thing in her father's household but had known he could not do so. He would have sent her to his own townhouse, was it not shut up and empty of servants, for he had sent them all to his country estate to clean it from top to bottom before preparing it for his mother and sister.

That was not a conversation he was looking forward to having.

His mother, widowed and sad, would have to face the difficult reality that she would now be expected to vacate her own home in order to reside in the smaller estate Gideon had called his own for so many years. It was not something Gideon would push upon her, of course, particularly not when she was still grieving, but he had very little intention of bringing Georgina to live with him as his wife, only for his mother to reside there also. As for his sister, not yet out, he hoped that she would soon find herself a suitable husband or that she would be willing to consider relocating also. Again, it was not something Gideon expected to demand of her but it would be put to her gently, reminding her that a good many things were now to change. He was to be wed in a few months' time, once the banns were called, and would have to ensure that his new home was ready and waiting for them both.

It would be strange, of course, to now seat himself in

his father's study, where he had so many fond memories of spending time with the good gentleman. His father had never been outwardly expressive with his emotions but Gideon had always known that his father loved him very deeply. He had done all he could to prepare Gideon to take on the title when the time came, and Gideon's deepest regret was not being by his father's side when he had taken his last few breaths.

"I do hope the fever has not reached here," Georgina said, breaking the silence that had fallen between them. "After all, part of the reason we are coming here is to remove ourselves from that *dreadful* city."

Gideon gave her a tight smile. "I do hope not, "he replied, realizing that, yet again, Georgina was displaying her inability to consider anyone but herself. "There has been a good deal of suffering already and one can only hope that it will come to an end very soon."

Georgina sniffed delicately. "I must keep myself as far away from those who are ill, of course. Father would be in such a terrible state of distress if he were to hear news that I was ill."

Georgina's father was to return from London to his country seat, whilst Francis escorted Georgina and her lady's maid to his own estate for a prolonged stay. "I am quite sure you can write to reassure him almost the moment you are received," Gideon replied, with a little harshness to his tone. "All will be well, Georgina. I am quite sure of it."

However, upon arriving at the Dunstable estate,

Gideon had the distinct impression that all was not well at all. The butler appeared very late indeed, for the carriage had been sitting for a good few minutes before anyone came to assist them. There were only two footmen, when Gideon was quite sure they had at least six.

"Jones," he said firmly, walking towards the butler as Georgina was assisted down from the carriage by one of the footmen. "Where is everybody? What the devil's going on?"

Jones the butler, looked rather harried. "Your mother is asking for you, my lord," he said, a little stiffly. "Please do hurry. She will tell you all, I am sure. Shall I escort you both to the drawing room?"

Rather perturbed by all of this, Gideon took Georgina's hand, placed it on his arm and walked with her up the steps into the house.

His breath caught at the state of the place. The windows were grubby, the marble floor was clearly stained and it looked as though the place had not been cleaned in a good many days. Making to say something, he saw the butler's pained expression and chose to close his mouth, recalling that the butler had promised that his mother could explain it all.

"Good gracious, Dunstable!" Georgina cried, as they walked towards the drawing room. "I have visited here on more than one occasion and I have never seen it look in such a dire state as it is today. Whatever has happened?"

Gideon cleared his throat. "I cannot say," he said, firmly. "Mama is waiting for us both, however, and I am quite sure –"

He was cut off by the sound of his mother's voice reaching him, the drawing room door being flung open.

"Dunstable? Is that you?"

The thin figure of his mother stepped out into the hallway and, dropping Georgina's hand, Gideon took his mother's hands in both of his, greeting her warmly.

"Mama," he murmured, looking at her with concern as he took in the paleness of her cheeks and the sadness in her eyes. "Something has happened, has it not? Why is the estate so unkempt?"

Lady Dunstable shook her head silently and gestured towards the drawing room. Growing more and more afraid by the minute, Gideon walked with her inside with Georgina at his heels.

"A tea tray, my lord?" the butler asked, now looking a little less harassed. "Or the brandy tray?"

Georgina shot him a hard glance but Gideon disregarded her. "One of both, if you please," he said, firmly. Georgina had always made her dislike of liquor more than apparent to him but he had always ignored it. On a day like this, he felt as though he would require more than one stiff drink.

"Very good, my lord. And may I say it is good to have you back with us."

The butler withdrew but not before Gideon had spotted the flash of relief that crossed his face. All the more perturbed, he turned his attention back to his mother, who was still holding his hand tightly.

"Mama," he said kindly, leading her towards a chair by the fire and seating her down. "What is it? What has occurred?"

His mother choked back a sob. "Oh, Dunstable! You have only been gone but ten days and everything has gone terribly wrong. I am afraid, so afraid."

Georgina cleared her throat. "Afraid, Lady Dunstable?" she asked, a slight note of fear in her voice. "But why? What is there to be afraid of?"

Gideon did not take his eyes from his mother. "Mama, what has gone wrong?"

She pulled out a small lace handkerchief from her pocket and dabbed at her eyes. "One of the servants, a maid, became sick."

A gasp from Georgina caught Gideon's ears, just as his stomach dropped to his toes.

"Your sister insisted that we send many of the staff away, continuing their pay until it was safe to return," Lady Dunstable continued. "You know Francine has always had the kindest of hearts." A small, tremulous smile caught her lips. "I did not know what to do but it appears that she was correct to do so. The maid, I am afraid to say, was not long for this world." A sob escaped her. "She died of the fever, Dunstable."

Gideon swallowed hard, fear racing through him. "The fever?" he asked, hoarsely. "Scarlet fever?"

Lady Dunstable looked up at him. "That is what the doctor said when I sent for him. There are some loyal staff who would not go when we asked – Jones, the butler, a footman and a maid or two. We could not have done without them but this is why you see your estate as it is now." Her eyes were fixed on his, an almost begging expression on her face. "Did I do right in allowing your

CHAPTER 2   23

sister to follow this course of action?" she asked, her voice breaking. "Did I, Dunstable?"

He caught her hands again and pressed them tightly. "Indeed, mama. The fever is passed quickly and I would not want any of my staff to become ill." He looked into her eyes, seeing signs of tiredness and strain but none of sickness. "You are quite well, then?"

His mother nodded. "I am."

"And Francine?" Gideon said, wondering where his sister had gone to. "Where is she?"

His mother shook her head sadly. "She is gone to give food and medicine to the tenants, Dunstable. I could not stop her. One of the tenant families has a child that is unwell. Your sister would not be prevented from going to her aid." A slight shrug lifted his mother's shoulders. "I wanted to protect her but she insisted on departing to go to them and I knew, in my heart, that you would have done the same had you been here. You are both strong-willed and kind of heart."

Georgina shot to her feet, breaking the tender moment. "I cannot linger here."

Gideon looked at her, not in the least bit surprised. "Georgina, it is not as bad as you think. The servants are –"

"The servants are gone!" Georgina exclaimed. "I am not about to start getting onto my hands and knees to clean floors, if that is what you are thinking Gideon!"

"No, indeed not," he said, soothingly. "But -"

"And how will we eat?" Georgina continued, gesturing wildly. "I cannot exactly go out and pluck a chicken or milk a cow! What is it you are intending to do, Gideon?"

Lady Dunstable rose to her feet. "My dear Georgina," she said, in a soft yet rather firm voice. "We have managed quite well thus far. Where is it you intend to return to, when this fever, this disease, seems to be everywhere?"

This unsettled Georgina for a moment, for she clasped her hands in front of her and did not quite know how to answer. A moment or two passed before his fiancée shrugged and made her way to the door. "I shall return to London to ensure I can travel back home with father. He had no immediate plans to leave the town and so I am quite sure I can return in time to travel back with him." She shot Gideon a fierce look. "Really, Dunstable, you cannot expect me to remain here under these circumstances!"

Gideon gritted his teeth. "No, indeed not, Georgina," he muttered, slowly getting to his feet so as to accompany her to the door. "I would never once have suggested that you think of others instead of simply yourself. I would never have imagined you to show any kind of care or consideration for the difficult circumstances of another."

Georgina gasped, her eyes rounding.

"Dunstable, really!" she exclaimed, flouncing down the hallway as he unwillingly followed her. "You are being quite ridiculous, Dunstable. I do not wish to remain here and assist in what is an already laughable situation. You cannot expect me to linger within your estate when I do not so much as have a maid to tend to me!"

Gideon did not point out that she had her own lady's maid with her, knowing that it was utterly useless to argue with her. Georgina always did what she thought best and he should not expect her to show any sort of consideration or care for others. After all, that was not who he knew her to be.

"You will have to give my men some time to prepare the carriage again," he said, pulling open the door and stepping outside onto the steps. "And may I suggest you recall your lady's maid and your things, which I am sure have already been taken up to your bedchamber. I will go and see the carriage is readied for you within the hour."

Georgina gaped at him. "But, Dunstable," she exclaimed, her cheeks paling. "I did not think you would be lingering here also. Are you not returning to London with me?"

The very idea made his stomach turn over. "No, Georgina, I am not," he replied, tersely. "I have a family here that requires my aid."

"But you have a sick servant here, Dunstable," Georgina continued, tears pooling in her eyes. "It is not safe."

He grimaced. "Nor is London. No, Georgina, I cannot and will not return with you. Now if you will excuse me, there is a great deal I must see to."

Turning away from her at once, he strode down the steps and across the graveled path towards the stables. Having given quick instructions to the men within – who nodded and said they would have to find fresh horses but that the carriage would be ready within the hour – he continued to make his way through his estate gardens until he reached the very outer edge.

The path was easy enough to find and Gideon walked with confidence, knowing exactly where he was going. Dodging under a few tree branches, he finally found his way and walked along the muddy path that led to the church and the graveyard.

Finally, where he had long wanted to be, he stopped just outside the graveyard gate for a moment, feeling his heart fill with heaviness. He missed his father.

The grave was not hard to find, given that it had one of the most prominent places in the churchyard. Gideon felt his heart break into a thousand pieces as he drew near it, wishing that he had made it home in time to see and speak to his father one last time.

"Father," he whispered, as though somehow, in some way, his dear father could hear him. "Whatever am I to do?"

The truth was, despite doing his utmost to put a brave front forward, reassuring his mother that all would work out and that they would be able to pull together in order to ensure things continued at the estate as they had been, Gideon felt as though he were walking on shaky ground. He was entirely unsure as to whether or not they would, in fact, be able to continue on without servants and the like. For heaven's sake, he did not know how to cook a meal or, as Georgina had stated so clearly, find a way to bring in milk and the like! He bowed his head, silently thankful for the few servants who had remained at the Dunstable estate. Yet, within his thanks, there also came a slow lingering fear that the illness might pervade his home further. With one ill servant already abed in his house, there was no promise that the rest of them would evade the fever. What would he do if the few servants he had left then succumbed to it? What if his mother, his sister or even himself became ill? What would happen then?

"Help me," he groaned aloud, one hand brushing over his eyes in an attempt to keep himself grounded despite the tears pricking at his eyes. He felt entirely alone, lost and afraid whilst knowing he would have to present a sure and steady front to his mother, his sister, and his staff. He was the new Baron Dunstable, was he not? And that meant doing all he could to help the estate flourish, even in difficult times.

Drawing himself up, Gideon let out a long, steadying breath, his eyes on the headstone before him. "I do miss you, father," he admitted aloud, before turning on his heel and leaving the graveyard, knowing that there was work to be done.

CHAPTER THREE

Josephine hugged her thin shawl about her shoulders and began to hurry along the streets, wondering where the best place was to go to find a bed for the night. She knew there was a tavern in Smithfield Market and that the lady there was kind-hearted, and she wondered if there might be any opportunity there for her to get a good night's rest. As she quickened her steps, her gaze snagged on the rather ominous looking church that loomed before her.

Stopping, Josephine felt her heart quail, wondering if she ought to go in and pray for a time. She could pray for the disease that seemed to be taking so many lives and, at the same time, thank God for the kind gentleman who had brought her so much goodness.

"Careful there!"

Glancing over her shoulder, Josephine saw a young man staggering slightly as he knocked into another man.

He had one hand to his throat as if it pained him and his eyes were bright with fever.

Her heart leaped into her throat. This man was ill.

Her wrapped coins still held tightly in her hand, Josephine watched the young man try desperately to move towards the church, his feet stumbling along the pavement. He was not about to make it, she realized, not without help.

Her mind screamed at her to take her money and go on her way, but her heart could not simply see his suffering and turn away. She had already had the fever and had recovered, but there were so many who would not. She was not afraid of the disease for her own sake but hated the way it claimed so many lives. Could she really allow it to claim another, when she was standing there, able to help?

Shoving her wrapped coins deep into her pocket and praying that she would not lose them, Josephine hurried towards the young man.

"You are not well," she stated, holding onto his hand and putting one hand onto his forehead, feeling him hot. "Are you seeking refuge in the church?"

The man looked at her for a moment with eyes that were heavy with illness. "Help," he said, his voice rasping. "Here. Help is here."

Leaning on her heavily, Josephine had no other choice but to lead the man into the church, a little unsure as to what she would find there. Churches were, on the whole, places where help and aid could be found but with such a terrible disease ravaging the whole town, she was not sure there would be anyone within willing to do what they could.

"Hello?" she called, as she helped the young man inside. "Is there anyone here?"

A harassed-looking elderly man stepped forward, his eyes on the young man Josephine led in.

"The fever?" he asked, harshly. "Is it the fever?"

Josephine nodded. "It is."

"Come with me."

Somehow, they both managed to get the young man down a long flight of wooden steps that led into a dimly lit, rather murky basement. Josephine caught her breath, frozen at the sight that met her eyes and the sounds that crowded in her mind. There was nothing but people everywhere. People lying on makeshift beds, clearly in the grip of the fever. People struggling to breathe, children crying fitfully whilst their anxious mothers watched over them.

"What is this place?" she asked, hoarsely, as the elderly gentleman began to lead her and the young man into the corner of the room.

"Don't you know?" he asked, sounding a little surprised. "I thought, since you were bringing your brother here –"

"He's not my brother," Josephine interrupted, quickly. "I just saw him coming towards the church. He wouldn't have made it in here on his own."

The elderly gentleman paused for a moment, his eyes fixed on hers. "You have a kind heart, I think," he said, softly. "That is good of you, miss."

Josephine managed a small smile. "Josephine," she

said, as they helped the young man down onto a pile of hessian sacks in the corner. "I – I can help, if you need me here?"

She did not know where such an offer had come from, but neither could she simply stand here and look at all the sick folk without feeling the urge to help them. She knew she could easily move on and go to find herself a new place to live, away from the disease, but seeing the pain and the grief that existed here tugged at her heart. Turning away from them all now would be senseless.

"It be dangerous around here," the gentleman said in a low tone, as the young man tossed and turned on the floor beside them. "The fever takes almost everyone."

Josephine's mind immediately threw up images of her own parents as they struggled with fever, her gut twisting painfully. "I have already had it," she replied, softly. "I do not fear it."

The elderly gentleman seemed to understand. "For whatever reason, the good Lord has seen fit to spare me also," he replied, patting her shoulder. "I'm Sam. The good doctor you see over there is Doctor Thomas. The vicar stays in the church most days, doing as much praying as he can. The doctor here's a good man. He's doing all he can to help these folk but more just keep coming." Shaking his head, he sighed sadly. "There's a few more that help us, but they do the burying."

Josephine closed her eyes for a moment, grief rising up in her.

"You've lost a few loved ones?"

Her voice was barely audible. "My parents," she

replied, hoarsely. "I'm not from here. I mean, I came from Hampstead but the fever is worse here."

Sam nodded. "It is. It takes the young especially." His eyes were sad as he looked at her. "Are you certain you want to help us here, Josephine? It isn't a place of happiness."

"I know," Josephine replied immediately, feeling her resolve steadying. "But I want to help. Truly. What can I do?"

Sam smiled at her, looking relieved and grateful. "Let me just fetch Doctor Thomas over here to look at this young man and then I'll get him to talk to you."

Josephine watched quietly as Doctor Thomas looked over the young man on the pile of sacks, seeing the strain so evident on the doctor's face. He was pale and exhausted, evidence of his lack of rest.

"He is burning up," the doctor muttered, shaking his head.

"And he was holding his throat when I first drew near him," Josephine added gently. "That is what made me think he had the fever."

Doctor Thomas, whom Josephine thought to be younger than his lined face appeared, looked at her with resignation. "You have seen this fever, then?"

"I have endured it," Josephine replied, firmly.

The doctor gestured to the man's mouth. "You see this? This paleness here around his mouth?" His voice was devoid of emotion, as though he had separated himself entirely from what he had seen and experienced.

"It is the sign I always look for to make a sure diagnosis. This man has scarlet fever. It will progress quickly. The rash will appear on him very soon."

There was a subtle warning in his words but Josephine fought back her sudden jolt of fear. She had been through this once already and would not allow it to chase her away. "I want to help, sir. What can I do?"

The doctor shook his head. "I am doing what I can for them all, but with the vomiting, there is always a good deal that needs to be cleaned up." His eyes flickered to hers, questions deep within. "The patients need cool rags on their foreheads to attempt to keep their temperatures down. They require gruel if they can stomach it. I am attempting treatments with a solution of salts and nitrate silver, but it seems that it only helps some."

Sam cleared his throat. "If they make it past the ninth day, then we have a little more hope. Those patients are moved to the other end of the basement. The worst ones stay down here."

"We do not let the blood," the doctor continued, with a sharp look towards Josephine. "I know it is often common practice amongst those in higher society but these people here have nowhere else to go. They are weak and frail. To bleed them now and let them faint will, I believe, only make things worse. We treat them with what we have and do a good amount of praying."

Josephine looked back at the doctor steadily. "I can pray, sir." She felt her determination rise, desperate to do what she could to help these unfortunate people. "Have you vinegar and feverfew, Doctor Thomas?"

A slight frown flickered across the man's brow. "I do."

"My mother used to use it to help bring a fever down," Josephine replied, with a small smile. "Might I be permitted to make up a solution for the cool cloths?"

The doctor did not seem to be affronted by this suggestion in any way. "You are welcome to try anything," he said, calmly. "I have done as much as I can thus far although I am always eager to hear of any new treatments. Do whatever you wish with the vinegar and feverfew, Josephine. I will be glad for your help."

She smiled at him, her expression tinged with sorrow. "Thank you, sir. I will do whatever I can to help you. There are just so many of them." Her eyes drifted over the doctor's shoulder, looking at the prone form of so many patients, their bodies racked with suffering. "I can only hope it will be of some use."

Some hours later and Josephine felt exhausted. She had been given the freedom to use the vinegar and feverfew and had worked herself to the bone, rinsing the cloths in the concoction before placing them on the foreheads of those who were unwell. The little children she bathed or ensured that their mothers or sisters caring for them knew exactly what to do. The young man in the corner, the one she had helped bring inside, was no longer tossing and turning but rather appeared to have settled a little, although he was still hot to the touch.

Setting down her bowl, she rinsed his cloth again and patted it gently over his face before placing it back on his forehead. The young man groaned quietly but his eyes remained shut. Josephine closed her eyes and prayed silently for a moment, her heart aching for the loss and the grief and the death that surrounded her.

"The doctor is mighty pleased with you."

Looking up, she saw Sam standing to her left, looking at the man on the floor.

"Is he?" Josephine murmured, getting to her feet. "I'm glad I'm able to do something."

Sam lifted one eyebrow. "That mixture of yours seems to be helping a good few folks. I'm not saying the fever's gone from them but it does seem to be settling them a bit more. Just look at this chap here! He's not tossing and turning anymore."

Josephine let out a small sigh. "My mother used to treat folk in our village this way. She said it was always good at helping to bring down a fever."

"I'm sorry you lost her," Sam said, gently. "But for what it's worth, I'm glad you're here now, helping these folk. This fever is a terrible thing to endure."

Josephine nodded fervently. "It is," she said faintly, remembering the terrible ache in her throat and the dryness of her mouth and skin. "I do not know how I got through it when so many other folks are dying."

Sam shook his head. "Maybe it is so we can help," he said, with a slight shrug. "There aren't exactly a lot of folk here willing to come down to the Devil's basement to take care of the sick."

Something inside Josephine shuddered violently. "The Devil's basement?" she repeated, her voice trembling. "Is that what they call this place?"

Sam spread out a hand at the dark, gloomy basement filled with nothing but sickness and death. "Isn't that what it looks like?" he asked, with compassion showing on his face. "And yet you are here anyway. An angel sent to help the sick. That's what you are, Josephine, an angel. And angels can bring light and life."

Josephine struggled against the fears that began to tie themselves around her heart, knowing that what she had done with the vinegar and feverfew was only a very small part of battling the fever. "I hope so," she whispered, tears pricking at her eyes as another wail went up from the back of the basement. Another person gone. Another life taken. Another grave to dig. Another death here in the Devil's basement.

CHAPTER FOUR

"Jones?"

The butler turned at the sound of Gideon's voice, looking at him with fear in his eyes.

Gideon's stomach twisted. "Is he ill?"

"I'm afraid so, my lord," the butler said, hoarsely. "The doctor has been and prescribed the same thing as he did for Maisy, God rest her soul."

It had now been a fortnight since Gideon had returned home and things had grown steadily worse. Maisy, the maid taken ill with the fever, had subsequently died and had needed to be buried. Everything in her room had been burned, for that was thought to be one way to prevent the disease from spreading. Gideon had overseen it himself, whilst the butler had ensured that Maisy's room had been scrubbed from top to bottom. Gideon had prayed that this meant the disease wouldn't spread but now, it seemed, it had taken hold of his household.

This was the third footman sick and the only other maid left in the house was now rather pale – although Gideon could not tell whether that was from fear, exhaustion or illness.

"You had best go home, Jones," he said, thickly. "I will not have you ill also."

The butler drew himself up to his full height. "I will not leave your side, my lord."

Gideon shook his head, firmly. "No, Jones. You are a stalwart and I both respect and appreciate your willingness to do what you can to remain loyal to this family but I cannot have another person becoming ill simply from being in this house."

Jones shook his head. "I do not think I need fear this illness, my lord," he said, slowly. "I recall having such symptoms when I was a young man. The agony of it still lingers in my memory but perhaps in having it once, I will not have it again." Holding up one hand, he stopped Gideon's protest. "I insist, my lord. You need help and I am more than willing to give it. Please, allow me to do my duties, as I have done for so long. I am not afraid."

Gideon wanted to insist that Jones return to his small cottage just outside the estate and remain there until the fever no longer gripped his estate but he could tell from the look in the man's eyes that he was completely determined to remain no matter Gideon said.

"Very well," he said, heavily. "What does the doctor suggest for the footmen?"

Jones shook his head, his expression morose. "Just the same as Maisy," he said, slowly. "Cool cloths, broth and perhaps a bleeding if they do not improve."

Something twisted in Gideon's gut. "A bleeding did not help Maisy," he muttered, darkly. "It only appeared to weaken her all the more." The doctor had bled Maisy stating that it was to purify and cleanse, but Gideon had seen her weaken almost immediately after. Less than a day later, and she was gone.

"There are to be no blood lettings, Jones," he said, firmly. "We will do what we can to help them with the cloths and the broth but there is to be nothing else unless I permit it."

The butler looked a little relieved. "Very good, my lord. Will I make up the broth?"

Gideon, who had been relying on the kitchen maid for their somewhat meagre meals of late, lifted a brow. "You know how to make broth, Jones?"

A small smile caught the butler's lips. "I do, and may I say it is a very good broth, my lord," he replied, quickly. "I can bring some for yourself and the ladies also, if you would enjoy it with the cold meats and cheeses that have been set aside for dinner this evening?"

"I would be most grateful," Gideon replied, firmly, despite the fact that his dinners of late had been very different to what he was used to. "You are a marvel, Jones. Remind me to increase your wages."

"Should I survive, my lord, then I will ensure I do just that," the butler replied, a touch morbidly, before making his way towards the kitchens.

Gideon sighed heavily for a moment before picking up the tea tray and making his way back up the servants' staircase and towards the drawing room. His mother was growing more and more weary every day and his sister, Miss Francine Peters, had finally been convinced to stop going out to the tenant's homes so often when they required her help here. Of course, it had been profoundly difficult for the three of them to adjust to such a change in their circumstances and in what was required of them but Gideon was proud of the way both his mother and sister had faced their difficulties without question.

"Mama?"

He walked into the drawing room and set the tea tray down in front of the fire, seeing his mother's lined face weary in the firelight.

"You are tired, mama," he said gently, handing her a cup of tea. "You must rest."

His mother let out a quiet laugh. "I cannot rest, Dunstable, not now. Not when there is a crisis."

Gideon frowned, looking into his mother's face and seeing her flushed cheeks. "Are you feeling quite all right, mama?" he asked, carefully. "You are not feeling ill, are you?"

Lady Dunstable did not immediately respond. "I – I am feeling a little chilled, that is all," she said after a moment or two. "I thought to sit close to the fire in order to ward the cold away. I am quite sure I am just rather tired, that is all." Her smile, however, did not reach her eyes and there was something about her expression that told Gideon he needed to watch her carefully.

"You need not do anything other than sit here for the rest of the day," he said, quietly. "Promise me you will not move from this seat until I return."

She laughed tiredly, pressing his hand with fingers that were warm on his own. She was so glad to have him back from London. "Of course, Dunstable, if you insist. Where are you going?"

"I must see to the horses," Gideon replied, feeling a little uneasy about leaving his mother alone. "Is Francine to join you soon?"

"Very soon," his mother replied, evidently aware of his concern. "She insisted on banking the fires in both my bedchamber and her own, although how she has learned what to do is quite beyond me!"

A small chuckle escaped Gideon, thinking fondly of his sister with her determined spirit. "Because Francine will simply try and try and try until she succeeds at whatever she is doing, no matter how much it costs her." He rose to his feet, his concern for his stubborn sister and exhausted mother still ringing through him. "You will encourage her to sit for a time, will you not?"

"Of course," his mother replied with a smile. "Go and see to the horses, Gideon. We will be quite all right until you return."

Gideon made his way outside, drawing in a long breath of fresh air and letting it fill his lungs. Looking up at the sky, he took in the blue, the wisps of cloud floating across the sky and the birds that were flying from one place to the next. No-one would guess that this place was struggling with the fever, not in such an idyllic circumstance. And yet, there was more fear and death and darkness within him than he had ever felt before.

"My lord, you have a letter."

Jerking in surprise, Gideon turned to see the butler hurrying towards him, a sealed note in his hand. "Thank you." Jones nodded and made to turn away.

"How are the footmen?"

The butler hesitated. "I cannot tell, my lord," he replied, honestly. "They are all taking some broth and the cloths appear to be doing their part in helping settle their fever but there is no great change, I'm afraid." He turned his head. "Should I send for the doctor again?"

Gideon reaction was instant. "No, indeed not," he said, firmly. "The man will only want to bleed them and I will not have it. Not after what happened with Maisy."

"Very good, my lord." The butler left him alone to read the letter which he knew at once to be from Georgina. The seal broken, he unfolded it quickly and began to read.

'Dunstable', it began. 'I have returned to London only to find my father gone to his country seat already. I have written to him and expect the carriage to be sent for me forthwith. I have a few staff, my lady's maid and my companion still here so I will be glad to wait.'

"Foolish girl," Gideon muttered aloud, frustrated that she had returned to London without making certain that her father would still be there. "She ought to have waited here until a letter could be sent."

There was more to the letter.

'I do not wish to see you, Dunstable, not until you are sure the illness has left your estate,' Georgina continued. 'The fever continues to rage through London but I am certain I am quite safe within my father's house. Do not come for me, I pray you. Once the illness has cleared from your home then I should be glad to stay for an extended visit, as I had initially intended. Yours, Georgina.'

It was a fairly short letter but certainly direct. Gideon had not expected anything less, for he knew Georgina was nothing more than a self-indulgent young lady who, in spite of her foolishness was most likely afraid of the fever sweeping through the realm. He could well understand that.

Making his way to the stables, Gideon crumpled up the letter and placed it firmly in his pocket, finding that he did not particularly care whether or not Georgina was to return to him or not. The truth was, he had never felt anything for the lady, and certainly had never had even a moment of true affection for her. They were to be married, yes, but it was a marriage based on suitability and family ties rather than anything else. He had always expected such a thing, given that he was to be a titled lord of the realm and so had never allowed himself to yearn for or even think of anything else.

For whatever reason, his mind traveled back to the young lady he had met in town, recalling her big beautiful eyes that seemed overly large in her thin, drawn face. His heart swelled in sympathy for her all over again, wondering if she was still alive, or whether she had succumbed to the fever like so many others.

"Here we go."

It was just as well that he enjoyed being around his horses, for to feed them, groom them and even muck the stalls out did not seem to Gideon to be much of a labor. In fact, he almost relished it. It forced him to stop worrying about all that was going on around him, forced him to concentrate simply on what he was doing rather on what might happen to his estate and his family if the fever continued to spread. He did not know how many hours had passed but it certainly felt like a long time before he stopped and stretched tall, his back a little painful from where he had been bending with the shovel.

"There we are," he said to his pride and joy, the dark stallion in the corner stall. "All safe in here, are we not?"

The stallion, Hunter, snuffled his pocket in an attempt to find some sugar but Gideon only laughed and rubbed Hunter's velvety nose. Sighing heavily to himself, Gideon lingered in the stables for another moment or two before pulling his coat back on to step outside into the cold evening air.

"Gideon!"

He jerked his head around to see Francine running towards him, her skirts flying in the wind. Her face was sheet white and he caught her hands, hearing her gasp for air.

"What is it?" he asked at once, dread running all through him. "What is wrong, Francine?" He was terribly afraid that another one of his staff had died, or that Jones the butler had suddenly succumbed, despite his belief that he might miss it altogether.

"You must send for the doctor!" Francine cried, beginning to drag him towards the house. "It is Mama."

Gideon stopped dead, his whole body frozen in place. "Mama is ill?" he asked, hoarsely. "Are you sure?"

Francine nodded, tears in her eyes. "I had to put her to bed myself, Gideon, even though she continued to insist that she was quite well. She is burning with fever and yet protesting that she is cold!" Her fingers tightened on his, fear running all through her expression. "Her throat aches, Gideon. Her throat!"

He could not move, could not speak for a full minute, realizing that the worst thing he had imagined was now coming to pass. His own mother was ill with the fever.

"You *must* go for the doctor," Francine cried, tugging him again. "Please, Gideon, you must go now! She must be cared for."

"No."

Gideon spoke slowly, his voice thick with emotion.

"No, I will not send for the village doctor, Francine. I cannot, not after what he insisted upon doing to Maisy."

Francine's eyes widened. "Then what will you do, Gideon?"

He paused for a moment. "I think I must return to London to fetch someone from there," he said, slowly. "Someone who has dealt with the illness and knows precisely what they must do. Jones, our butler, knows everything that our village doctor has prescribed for the servants that have been taken by the fever. He will guide you. I must find someone else, someone who will not insist on bleeding her, someone who has something *else* to try. London is the only place I can go where I might be able to find someone like that."

A ragged sob escaped Francine. "But Gideon, that will take you some days."

"And yet it is the best I can do for our mother," he insisted, hating the idea of leaving them both but knowing he had very little choice. "Jones knows what to do in order to help Mama as much as he can until I return from town." Putting his hands onto Francine's shoulders, he looked into her eyes and tried to hold his gaze steady. "It will mean leaving you to deal with things here, until I return," he said, quietly, knowing just how much he was asking of her. "I will be, at the very most, only four days gone." He winced inwardly, knowing just how quickly the fever could take a hold. "But I will go almost this very moment if you feel you are able to remain here."

Francine held his gaze, her lip quivering as her blue eyes, so like his own, blinked back tears.

"Yes," she said, hoarsely. "Yes, I can do it. Go then, Gideon. Go now. I will remain here with Jones and Mama."

"Thank you." He kissed her cheek, squeezed her hands and stepped away, hurrying back towards the stables he had only just come from. His stallion was ready and waiting, snorting eagerly as Gideon threw the saddle onto his back. He would have to change horses at least once on his ride to London but he knew an inn where he could do so. He had no intention of resting or remaining anywhere overnight, praying that the moon would be bright so that he could continue his journey onwards through the dark hours of the night.

Buttoning his coat, he placed one foot in the stirrup and threw his leg over the saddle, urging Hunter forward out onto the gravel path.

"I will not be long," he whispered, as though his mother could hear him. "Be strong, mama." Urging Hunter into a gallop, he soon left the Dunstable estate behind him, terrified that by the time he returned with the doctor, it would be too late.

CHAPTER FIVE

Josephine leaned her head back against the cold stone wall of the church, drinking in the air and letting her eyes adjust to the midday sunshine, even though it was something of a gloomy day. Her heart was heavy, her spirits low. She felt as though she carried death with her everywhere she went, as though the stink and the stench of it clung to her clothes and even her skin.

She had been working alongside the doctor for some weeks now and whilst there were some who had recovered, there were many more who had died. Each time, she had felt herself crumple with exhaustion and grief, the memory of her own parents coming back to her with full force – only for her to straighten her shoulders, rise tall and force herself to keep going.

There was no other choice. She could not continue on in her misery and pain, not when there were those who needed her. Doctor Thomas seemed to be pleased with her, and Sam kept on encouraging her whenever he could, but especially on difficult days.

Today was a difficult day.

Closing her eyes, Josephine forced herself not to become lost in the memories of her past. She did not want to think of what she had lost, not when so many people had lost loved ones, just as she had. She could see the grief in them, a shared understanding that was in their eyes. Whenever she met someone new, there was that flash of sympathy in their eyes, sympathy that told her they knew precisely what it was like to be left alone on this earth, separated from those you loved. The fever took anyone and everyone, old and young, wealthy or poor. They all came here, now. Here or to the other fever wards, set up wherever there was space.

Josephine sniffed the air, catching the faint scent of burning. Closing her eyes, she let out a long sigh. That was a regular occurrence around here these days. If someone died from the fever, everything they'd touched was burned, but it did not seem to make much of a difference. Those who had lived with the sick person often seemed to catch the fever soon after, and the process would begin all over again.

She rubbed her arms, glad for the new clothes that the doctor had found for her. They were not threadbare or torn, her feet encased in warm stockings and sturdy shoes that kept her from stepping into the vomit that was so often on the floor of the basement. Small mercies, she thought to herself, gratitude rising her in despite the desperation of her circumstances.

"Is this the Devil's basement?"

Josephine opened her eyes and saw a slightly older lady looking down at her, her face a little pale.

"Yes," Josephine replied, scrambling to her feet and feeling the same heaviness enter her soul. Was this to be another one sick? Another one she would have to tend, not knowing whether or not they would live or die? "Are you unwell?"

"No," the lady replied, with a slight frown. "I – I have had the fever and have recovered."

Josephine's eyes flared with a sudden understanding. "As have I."

"I – I know," the lady replied. "My name is Geraldine Easton. There are four of us here – myself included - who want to help you."

For a moment, Josephine did not understand. "Help me?" she repeated, slowly. "Four of you?"

"Yes." Geraldine Easton smiled a little carefully. "You might not need us, of course, but we wondered if there was something we could do."

Josephine stared at her, her spirits suddenly lifting, renewed and wonderful.

"We be maids in Lord Falconer's house, but he's sent us all away for a time," Geraldine continued, still looking a little uncertain. "I got ill soon after but the other three, they all cared for me and not one of them has the fever. I think they said they might have already had it or some such thing, but it's been a few weeks now and we're all as healthy as we can be." She tipped her head, looking at Josephine carefully. "Is it really terrible down there?"

Tears were putting an ache in her throat. "Yes," she replied, her voice shaking. "Yes, it is terrible. Much more than you would think." Praying that she hadn't set this good-hearted lady against the idea of helping simply by being honest, Josephine spread her hands. "But we're struggling with the number of people that come in. If you're truly wanting to help us, then I know we could use you all. In fact, we'd be more than grateful."

Geraldine smiled but her eyes remained grave. "Then I'll just go fetch the others. We'll come in straight away."

"Thank you." Josephine's voice was barely louder than a whisper, such was her gratitude and she held onto the lady's hands for a moment, feeling her burden lift for just a moment. "You can't know what this means."

Three days later and the work was still hard, the loss and the pain still terrible but yet there was something about having extra folk involved that helped Josephine to manage the constant requirements that were asked of her. Doctor Thomas had been just as overwhelmed as she had been, thanking each of the ladies in turn. He had suggested that if someone had already had the terrible disease, then they would not be likely to catch it again – which had brought a great deal of reassurance to Josephine and to the rest of her new friends.

The five of them worked steadily, with Sam pitching in to help wherever he could. The girls learned quickly what to do and Josephine no longer felt so alone in her duties. When there was a loss, they comforted each other, helping one another to find the strength to keep going. When there was tiredness, someone came to insist they rest, when there was hunger, someone brought food. Josephine worked as hard as she could, feeling herself filled with sorrow and, occasionally, when the illness was beaten and the person emerged from the fever, she let her heart fill with joy.

She could not let her spirits sink into despondency, not when she knew she had to keep going in order to bring as many people through the fever as she could. The vinegar and feverfew helped to prevent the temperature from rising, but aside from that, she could only do what the doctor told her, giving the sick either gruel or broth to drink as well as administering the various medicines Doctor Thomas handed her. On occasion, he gave laudanum to those who were suffering the most, trying his utmost to let them find a little peace whilst their bodies decided what to do next – to keep fighting or to give up completely. It was both a blessing and a curse, for so often it seemed to be the peace the person required simply to slip away into the next life. It tore at Josephine's heart each and every time it occurred.

"You are doing marvelously well," Sam murmured in her ear, as she wrung out the cloths for what seemed to be the hundredth time that day. "Doctor Thomas is ever so pleased with you. I doubt we'd have managed to keep this place going without you. And now look, you've managed to bring in four other women to help." His eyes shone with admiration and a renewed hope. "I always said you were an angel, Josephine."

"You're too kind, Sam," Josephine replied, quietly. "You do just as much as I do."

"When I can," Sam grunted, clearly well aware of his

own failing health. "My old bones like to complain whenever they can."

She let out a quiet laugh and made to turn away, only to hear the sound of Doctor Thomas' raised voice.

"Goodness," she murmured, as Sam came to stand a little closer. "Is Doctor Thomas arguing with someone down here?"

Sam frowned. "It surely can't be someone unwell," he muttered, his eyes glinting in confusion. "We're busy, yes, but Doctor Thomas doesn't send anyone away."

Josephine moved forward, a little confused and yet interested to know who it was arguing with Doctor Thomas. The voice sounded vaguely familiar and, as the men came into view, she felt another stab of recognition.

It was the gentleman who had helped her all those weeks ago, the gentleman who had given her what was more than enough to live on simply for showing him the way to his fiancée's home. She closed her eyes struggling to remember his name.

"Baron Dunstable," she said aloud, moving forward with purpose. "Whatever is the matter?"

She saw Baron Dunstable gesture wildly, whilst Doctor Thomas shook his head sadly, but with a steely glint in his eye.

"Might I be of any help?"

Doctor Thomas looked at her for a moment, something flickering in his expression. Baron Dunstable also looked at her but there was no immediate recognition in his expression. Josephine felt a small wave of disappointment wash over her but she immediately shrugged it away, knowing she was being foolish.

"Ah, Josephine," Doctor Thomas said, rubbing his forehead with the back of his hand. "This is Baron Dunstable. He is asking me to return with him to his estate in order to tend to his mother."

A wave of concern washed over Josephine, even though she did not know the lady in any way. "She has the fever?"

"Yes," Lord Dunstable replied, sounding frantic with worry. "I have searched London for a full day already, desperate to find a doctor able and willing to return with me but none have been able to do so. I must return this very afternoon but I cannot go back without some help. Please, we are all quite alone."

"Do you not have a village doctor?" Josephine asked, seeing Lord Dunstable frown immediately. "Can he not help you?"

"No," Lord Dunstable replied, fiercely. "He has bled one of my maids already and she died only a few hours later. He has no idea of what else to do and I will not allow him near my mother."

Doctor Thomas sighed. "That is the problem with these country doctors, Lord Dunstable. So many of them are poorly trained and have very little skill but who else can the village folk turn to?"

Lord Dunstable turned back to the doctor, sounding a little more hopeful. "Then will you come with me?"

Gesturing to the sea of people lying across the Devil's basement, Doctor Thomas shook his head. "I cannot leave these people, Lord Dunstable. More of them come in every day and the fever wards are already full. I have people to help me now, which is an astounding blessing given the danger of it all, but I cannot simply turn my back and leave it to them to deal with."

Lord Dunstable closed his eyes. "Please," he said, hoarsely. "I need someone."

"I will go with you."

Josephine clamped her mouth shut but it was much too late. The words had already left her lips and she found herself staring into the eyes of Lord Dunstable whilst Doctor Thomas, after a moment of thought, began to nod slowly.

"You?" Lord Dunstable exclaimed, waving a hand. "A scrap of a thing? I highly doubt you can –"

"I would watch what you say, Lord Dunstable," Doctor Thomas warned, interrupting the man. "This young lady, Josephine, has done more for these people than anyone. She has helped me in ways I did not expect. It was she who gave me the tonic to help bring the fever down and it has been more successful than I ever expected. She knows everything there is to know about the fever and how I treat it." He smiled at Josephine, who felt her stomach cramp nervously. "I can give you the medicines to take with you. You know what doses to give and when."

Josephine nodded slowly, suddenly feeling very nervous about leaving London and traveling with Lord Dunstable, who still did not recognize her and certainly didn't seem at all convinced that she would do in the place of Doctor Thomas given the scrutinizing look on his face.

"I hardly think that a woman can take the place of a

doctor," Lord Dunstable muttered, shaking his head. "Come now. Surely there must be someone else."

Josephine lifted her chin. "Either I go with you, Lord Dunstable or no-one does. Surely you cannot expect the good doctor to leave all of these sick folk behind simply to go to the aid of one of the nobility. Their lives are of equal importance, are they not?"

Lord Dunstable, to her surprise, now appeared rather ashamed. "Yes, of course," he said, dropping his head. "I would not like you to think that I cared nothing for these poor people."

This answer satisfied Josephine, aware that the gentleman was, in fact, simply desperate for help for his ailing mother. She recalled just how kind he had been to her, how he had spoken kindly to her and felt her heart soften.

"Do you think you can spare me, Doctor Thomas?" she asked, turning to the man who had become something of a friend these last few weeks. "I should have asked you first, of course."

Doctor Thomas studied her for a moment, thinking hard. "I think, Josephine, that this is the best solution for everyone involved. I would not want to let you go had you not found four others to come and help me." He reached for her hand and held it for a moment, and Josephine felt her heart lurch in her chest. "You will come back to the Devil's basement though, won't you? Once you are no longer required to help Lord Dunstable?"

There was not even a moment of hesitation. "Of course I will come back to help you," Josephine replied at once. "Thank you, Doctor Thomas."

CHAPTER 5 57

He shook his head, patting her hand. "Thank you, Josephine, for all you have done here. I know Sam and I will both miss your caring hand." A small smile caught his lips. "Once this is over I would like to make sure you are taken care of, for the kindnesses you have shown, Josephine. Don't think that I intend to let you back out to wander the streets again. I have a small practice and could always use your continued help."

Her breath caught, her eyes widening. This had given her a hope for her future. "Thank you, Doctor Thomas. You are very kind."

Chuckling, he let go of her hand. "It is just to ensure you return," he replied, with a touch of mirth that was so absent from their present circumstances. "Now, let me go and see to your things. I will make up extra doses, just in case of more illness."

"I – I have three footmen already ill," Lord Dunstable interrupted, his face white and strained. "And a maid, although I do not know if she had the fever. She simply looked unwell."

The doctor frowned. "It often starts with the look of a person," he said, grimly. "I will make sure to have all you require, Lord Dunstable. Just give me an hour or so."

"Thank you," Lord Dunstable replied, relief etched across his features. "Thank you both, very much."

CHAPTER SIX

Gideon let out a long sigh and put his face in his hands as he stepped out of the Devil's basement, suddenly desperate for air. He had wasted so much time. It would be the full four days by the time he returned home, praying desperately that his mother still lived.

Sinking down onto his haunches, his back against the cold stone wall of the church, Gideon tried not to let fear rattle at him. He had someone, at least, although it was not the doctor he had promised his sister. Yet, Doctor Thomas seemed to have faith that this young lady, this scrap of a thing, would bring his mother just as much aid as he himself would, had he been able to come.

A hint of shame climbed up his spine, sending heat into his face. Josephine had asked, with a small tilt of her head, whether or not he had considered all these sick people here somehow less than his own mother, and his immediate answer had wanted to be yes. It was not because of his status, he told himself, but a part of him knew that it was almost ingrained within him – that he, being a baron, was worth more than those who worked in the fields and begged on the streets. It was something he was struggling to battle against, seeing that this devastating illness touched them all, regardless of class. Yes, he loved his mother desperately, but how many other mothers lay struggling on the floor of the Devil's basement? It was not right for him to demand that the doctor come with him, simply to tend to one patient when it was so very evident that his skills were required here.

Taking his face from his hands, Gideon drew in a steadying breath, feeling almost weak with fear. He wanted to leave immediately but was now forced to wait again, wait until the doctor had prepared his medicines for Josephine to take. The girl had, at least, looked at him with confidence, her green eyes bright with assurance. That, at least, gave him a little hope that she would know what to do when it came to his mother.

"Lord Dunstable?"

He looked up and saw Josephine standing in the doorway of the church, a cotton bag twisted in her hand.

"Miss....." He realized he had not even asked her name, a little unsure what a gentleman ought to refer to a young woman such as she.

"Miss Noe," she replied, firmly. "But I would prefer Josephine, my lord. At times like this, I think such things as the use of correct titles and the like a little.... superfluous."

Gideon raised an eyebrow, rather astonished to hear her speak in such an ostentatious manner.

"You do not remember me, do you?" she asked, her expression a little forlorn. "I thought....."

"Remember you?" Gideon asked, a little surprised. "No, I'm afraid I do not. Are you suggesting we have met prior to this?"

She looked at him for a long moment, her eyes now somewhat sad. "We have, my lord," she replied, carefully. "But I should not expect you to remember – although you did express your surprise at my speaking back then also."

"I – I did?" Gideon asked, struggling to remember. "I must apologize, Miss Noe, for forgetting our first meeting. Things have been rather difficult of late."

Her smile was sympathetic, bringing him a sense of relief. "I understand, my lord. And I don't mind repeating myself. I used to work as one of the maids in a great house near my home. The housekeeper was very kind to me and taught me a good deal. I think she wanted me to be a lady's maid one day."

Something began to niggle at his mind.

"Not that the position lasted all that long," she continued, her eyes drifting away from his. "When my parents became ill I was forced to give it up entirely."

"And they have passed away," he said, slowly, a memory beginning to come back to him. "You came to London in search of work and then could not find any."

Her eyes flickered with grief. "Yes, that's right. Do you remember me now?"

He nodded slowly, amazed to see that this young lady from the streets had now subsequently transformed herself despite the horrendous situation she had been working in. Her hair was tied neatly back from her face, instead of blowing across her face. Her eyes were bright, her expression resolute, instead of the fear and terror that had splashed across her features when he had first spoken to her. Her dress and shawl did not have holes or tears, and her feet were no longer bare. It was little wonder he had not recognized her.

"You appear in much better circumstances now," he said, before flushing as he realized what he had suggested.

To his surprise, Josephine laughed, albeit rather sadly. "Indeed. The Devil's basement is better than the cold London streets, is it not?"

A slight frown caught his brow. "I gave you money, did I not?"

Her green eyes narrowed slightly. "Yes you did, my lord. You were very kind to me."

"Then, may I ask," Gideon continued, a trifle confused, "why you are working here, in the Devil's basement? I would have thought that, with the money I gave you, you would have been able to find a place of your own. There was more than enough for you –"

She held up one hand, stemming the flow of words from his lips. "You have been inside the Devil's basement, my lord. How can you ask me such a thing?"

Staring at her for a moment, Gideon felt his shame flare. "You have a good heart, Miss Josephine," he muttered, realizing that the girl had given up the future she could have had with the money he had given her, simply to come here and help those who were in desperate need.

Josephine looked back at him steadily, a faint hint of

disappointment in her eyes. "My lord, I could not turn my back on these people. I have lost loved ones to the fever and I wanted to do what I could to help. That's why I am here."

He nodded, looking away from her. "I see."

"I *can* help your mother," she said, firmly, aware that he still was a little unsure as to how she might be able to help. "I have learned all I can from Doctor Thomas."

"And how many people have recovered?" he asked, desperation beginning to fill him. "How many have you seen manage to overcome this dreadful illness?" He searched her face, seeing her lips thin for a moment, evidence of just how much she hated the disease.

"Many have died," she admitted, quietly. "But many have lived as well. The young and the aged seem to be taken the most often – but you must recall, my lord, that these people live in squalor compared to you. They are often weak and ill already."

This did not give him a great amount of hope but, seeing that he had very little choice other than to agree, he nodded and led her towards the carriage he had managed to hire. "Then it seems I must put all of my hope in you, Miss Josephine," he murmured, opening the door and gesturing for her to sit inside. "We will make our way at once and I do not expect to stop particularly often."

He made to close the door, only for her to grasp his hand for a moment. Heat shot up his arm and he stepped back, looking at her in confusion.

"Where is your driver, my lord?" she asked, a little puzzled.

CHAPTER 6

Clearing his throat, Gideon shrugged. "I have no driver. Not one person could be spared from the estate. I will do it myself."

A slight rise of her eyebrows told him that she was rather astonished by this but, to his very great relief, she said not another word, allowing him to close the door. Doing so at once, he quickly attempted to climb up into the driver's seat, all the more embarrassed that it took him more than one attempt before he was seated carefully in the driver's seat. Picking up the reins, he held them carefully in his hands and flicked them once, then twice.

The horses did not move.

Frustrated, Gideon shook the reins again but still, the animals remained exactly where they were.

"Might you need some help, my lord?"

Closing his eyes, Gideon felt his face heat. "No, indeed, Miss Josephine," he replied, firmly. "I am quite capable, I assure you."

A quiet laugh caught his ears and his face burned all the hotter. Trying to push himself into action, he flicked the reins again, just as he would do if he were riding. It was not something he was used to, driving either a carriage or a phaeton, even though so many gentlemen possessed such a thing. He had never had the opportunity to drive a phaeton, since he had been overseas, and as such had very little experience in such matters.

"Might I try?"

He looked over his shoulder to see Miss Josephine standing on the pavement, her hands on her hips and her face tipped up to his.

"I said I can manage, Miss Josephine," Gideon replied, firmly. "Do go back inside."

She did not move. "You have not driven a carriage before, I think."

"*Please,*" he repeated, growing steadily angrier. "If you do not get in then I cannot drive the horses forward."

A slight lilt in her voice told him she was laughing at him. His frustration blew into anger, his expression furious as he turned his sharp eyes onto her. This was no laughing matter. He was trying to get back to his mother as quickly as possible and her refusal to climb back into the carriage was only making things all the more difficult.

"Now, see here!" he exclaimed, climbing down from his driver's seat with very little dignity or grace. "I am in a very great hurry and if you cannot see that, then I –"

"Oh, but I *can* see that, your grace," Miss Josephine interrupted, putting one hand on his arm. The simple touch seemed to take all of his anger away in a moment as Gideon felt it drain out of him and spread across the ground beneath his feet. "And, for what it is worth, I am trying to help."

Closing his eyes, Gideon let the last of his irritation blow away. "What is it you wish to do, Miss Josephine?"

There was a short silence. Gideon opened his eyes and looked back at her, seeing her green eyes warm as her smile spread gently. "I will drive," she replied, with a good deal of nonchalance. "After all, it is something I am well used to and I can assure you that, with your direction, we will arrive back at your estate very soon."

His mouth fell open. "Drive?"

She shrugged. "Why ever not?"

The embarrassment of the situation as it currently stood began to seep into his bones. "But you are –"

"A woman," she interrupted, irritably. "Yes, I am aware of that and, as you may well have noticed, my lord, quite capable. I can help your mother and I can drive your carriage. Now, are you going to allow me to do so or not?"

Gideon wanted to refuse at once, the shame of being driven through London by a woman whilst he sat inside screaming at his mind – but then the memory of his sister, white-faced as she begged him to go in search of help – began to tear at him. "You will freeze," he muttered, passing one hand over his eyes as any attempt to protest began to fall away. "You only have your shawl and –"

"Then may I have your coat?"

Blinking furiously, Gideon tried to answer but found the words dying in his throat. This lady was unlike any other he had met before, her lack of propriety breathtaking and yet refreshing in equal measure.

"May I?" she asked again, a trifle more gently. "It is very cold and if we are to make good time, I should not like to have to stop simply to warm up my frozen fingers – although I am quite used to those, I'm afraid."

Somehow, Gideon found himself shrugging out of his jacket and handing it to her, not quite sure what he was doing or why. Miss Josephine took it from him with a glad smile, leaving him standing in just his shirt and waistcoat.

"You'd best get into the carriage, my lord," Miss Josephine murmured, her small frame now wrapped in his coat, which was much too big for her. "Do excuse me."

As he stood there, still staring at her, she climbed deftly up into the driver's seat and took up the reins.

"My lord?"

Stammering for a moment, Gideon quickly gave her some directions and then clambered inside, sitting back against the velvet seat as he pulled the door closed. For a moment, he thought that Miss Josephine too would fail to have the horses moving but, almost as soon as he was comfortably seated, the crack of the reins was heard and the carriage immediately began to rumble away.

Closing his eyes, Gideon pushed away the last of his embarrassment and tried to concentrate on the fact that he would at least be returning to his estate with *someone* to help. He was still not quite sure what Miss Josephine could do but he had to hope that she had gleaned a good deal of knowledge from working with Doctor Thomas. He knew full well that this fever had already claimed a good many lives, both from the wealthy and from the poor. All he could do was pray that his mother would be spared and that Miss Josephine's ministrations would be effective. He had no other hope than her.

CHAPTER SEVEN

*J*osephine let go the reins, her fingers stiff and sore. She had not wanted to complain, knowing just how desperate Lord Dunstable was to return home. In addition, she had known that to delay would mean that Lady Dunstable could become all the worse, for every minute was precious.

"Here, let me help you."

She looked down from the driver's seat to see Lord Dunstable holding out his arms to her, wanting to help her down. For a moment, she wanted to refuse, to tell him that she could manage quite well on her own, but that would be foolish when she felt as though she were entirely frozen in her seat.

"You are cold," he said, his blue eyes filled with concern. Josephine felt her heart lift with warmth for a moment, feeling as though she meant something to him – only to realize that his concern for her wellbeing was simply due to his worry for his mother. If she was not well enough to care for Lady Dunstable, then he would be entirely alone.

"Yes, a little," she muttered, leaning forward and managing to place her cold hands on his shoulders. She felt her breath catch as his strong arms lifted her down, hating herself for her reaction to being so close to a handsome gentleman.

"Careful, there!" he exclaimed, as her knees buckled underneath her. "Goodness, Miss Josephine, you have almost done yourself in."

"I wanted to reach her as soon as possible," she said, gently, looking up into his face. "I can understand the fear that swirls about you."

His expression hardened for a moment and she thought he might turn away from her but, instead, he let out a long breath and nodded. "Thank you, Miss Josephine. That does bring me a little comfort." Supporting her still, he turned towards the house. "I'm afraid we will not be greeted by anyone – the staff are all unwell or have been sent away until the fever leaves my estate. If you can come inside, I will make sure to fetch us both some refreshments."

She leaned on his arm but felt warmth slowly returning to her limbs as they began to walk, her bones sore from her driving. "Your mother first, of course."

Lord Dunstable said nothing for a moment, glancing down at her with gratitude in his eyes. "Thank you, Miss Josephine."

"Miss Francine Peters, my sister."

CHAPTER 7

Josephine looked towards her, having had her gaze roving around the tall ceilings in astonishment, to see a tall, brown-haired young lady hurrying towards her – only to stumble as she did so.

Lord Dunstable let go of Josephine's arm at once and hurried towards his sister, leaving Josephine to catch up.

"Are you quite all right, Francine?" he asked, hoarsely, as the young lady put one hand to her chest. "Is Mama.....?"

"Mama is waiting for you," Miss Peters replied, her eyes drifting towards Josephine who immediately became concerned over the lady's pallor. "She is still in her bed and has been burning with fever for some days."

Josephine began to move forward at once, purpose driving her. "I will need a bowl and a few cloths," she said firmly, still a little worried over Miss Peter's pale face. "And some water."

Lord Dunstable nodded. "Of course. Let me take Francine – oh, Jones!"

Josephine saw a man approaching them, who, from his dress, she presumed to be the butler.

"This is Miss Josephine Noe," Lord Dunstable began, indicating Josephine with one hand. "She is come to help Mama – and the others, also."

Miss Peter's shot a doubtful look in Josephine's direction, whilst the butler appeared more than relieved.

"A woman?" Miss Peters asked, sounding quite surprised. "A woman is a doctor?"

Josephine did not take offense, knowing precisely why Miss Peters appeared so astonished. "I have been working with Doctor Thomas back in London, in Smithfield Market," she replied, calmly. "I may not be a doctor, Miss Peters, but I can assure you that I know everything that is to be done." Pausing for a moment, she considered what to say before continuing. "The fever is a difficult disease to treat, my lady. I will do all I can for your mother and for your staff also."

Miss Peters eyes filled with tears. "So you are not a doctor." She turned accusing eyes onto her brother, who reached for her hand. "Whatever are we to do, Dunstable?"

Josephine began to move past Miss Peters, having very little time to hear the lady complain and cry over the fact that Josephine was not, in fact, a doctor. The butler, who did not seem to have any concerns in the slightest, hurried her along the corridor.

"We must trust her, Francine," Josephine heard Lord Dunstable say, as she walked away. "I trust her. She knows what to do. I heard it from Doctor Thomas himself. Can you not be glad that we have *someone* here to help us? Or would you prefer I get the old village doctor and allow him to bleed our mother until she faints?"

A little relieved that at least Lord Dunstable was glad of her presence here, although it had taken him some time to trust she could do as good a job as Doctor Thomas, Josephine walked into a gloomy bedchamber where Lady Dunstable lay.

"There are staff ill also, you say?" she asked, looking up at the butler.

"Jones," he said, introducing himself. "Yes, there are.

CHAPTER 7

We have – I mean, we had – three footmen desperately ill. One, I'm afraid, has been lost to the illness."

Josephine's gut twisted.

"The other two are much the same," the butler continued with a heavy sigh. "There is a maid also and between the two of us, we have continued to keep the household running as best we can."

Her eyes narrowed. "And neither of you are suffering?"

Jones shook his head. "No, miss. Not as yet. I had the fever before, you see, and it doesn't seem to want to return to me."

A small smile tugged at Josephine's lips. "Nor me," she replied soberly, thinking of how lucky she was to have lived through the fever. "Then let me see to Lady Dunstable and then I will come below stairs."

The butler nodded, one hand reaching for her shoulder. "I am very glad you have come, Miss Josephine," he said, wretchedness in his voice. "I have been quite lost these last few days."

She smiled at him gently, seeing the worry in his eyes and knowing just how troubled he was. "Of course. I quite understand. You need not worry any longer. Please, a bowl, fresh cloths, and some water. As cold as you can get it."

He nodded, shot a glance to the prone form of Lady Dunstable and exited the room, leaving Josephine alone for a minute or two. She did not want to move forward to examine the lady until Lord Dunstable and his sister arrived but was already concerned by the musty air that sank into her lungs every time she took a breath.

"Miss Josephine."

Turning, Josephine saw Miss Peters come into the room to join her, a somewhat guilty expression on her face.

"I do apologize," she said, quietly, as Josephine listened in surprise. "I should have trusted that my brother did not bring someone back with him who would not know what to do." Miss Peters clasped her hands in front of her and bit her lip, her eyes still glassy. "I have been ever so worried."

Josephine nodded. "You have been alone with your mother some days, I understand," she said, gently. "I am here to help you as best I can. I have seen much sickness recently; Miss Peters and I know what to do to try and help."

Miss Peters shot her a sharp look. "Try?"

A sad smile crossed Josephine's face. She could not give Miss Peters false hope, not when she knew that the fever could be stronger than anything she could put against it. "I will be honest with you, Miss Peters. Scarlet fever is strong. It has taken many lives. I will do all I can for your mother, just as Doctor Thomas showed me. She is strong, your brother tells me, and that is in her favor." Reaching for Miss Peters hand, Josephine saw tears begin to run down Miss Peters face. "You are tired also, I think. You will need to rest."

"I will rest when my mother is better," Miss Peters replied, fiercely. "I cannot let her die. I – I love her."

Josephine felt a stab of pain, recalling just how much she had loved her own parents and how that love had not prevented them from being taken from her. "Of course," she managed to say, dropping Miss Peters hand. "Then, with your permission, I will examine her."

Miss Peters nodded. "Of course."

Josephine, however, did not first go to the lady in the bed but rather went to the window and drew back the drapes. The bright light made Miss Peters exclaim aloud but that did not stop Josephine. She pulled open the window, drawing in a full breath of fresh, clean air, so different to the London smog.

"But – is that not dangerous?" Miss Peters exclaimed, hurrying towards Josephine as though to shut the window again. "Surely my mother required darkness in order to rest."

Josephine stood directly in front of the window, putting her hands on her hips and looking at Miss Peters firmly in the eye. "No, my lady. Your mother requires fresh air and light." She recalled the gloominess of the Devil's basement and a shudder ran all through her. "I have seen the stench of death, Miss Peters, and I will not allow it to pervade here. Trust me, my lady. I know what your mother requires."

"Francine."

Miss Peters turned her head just as Lord Dunstable walked into the room, a tray in his hand.

"Francine, allow Miss Josephine to do what she thinks is best," Lord Dunstable said quietly, but in a voice that rang with firmness. "Come now, sit down by the fire. I have brought us all some tea."

Josephine's stomach rang hollowly at the sight of the biscuits and other small delicacies that lay on the tray in front of her, remembering how the butler had told her of the one kitchen maid that was left to run the house and finding herself incredibly grateful for the woman. "I must see to your mother first," she said, softly. "The butler is returning with what I require." A sudden thought hit her and she frowned. "Oh, but I have left my bag of supplies in the carriage."

Lord Dunstable set down the tray and nodded. "I will get it for you, Miss Josephine. Do excuse me. Francine, pour the tea and do take a drink. You look quite done in."

Miss Peters gave her brother a wan smile and set about doing what she had been asked, all the while casting suspicious glances towards Josephine. Josephine ignored this and pressed her hand against Lady Dunstable's forehead, feeling the heat that practically emanated from her. Her face was flushed with a paleness about the lady's lips and her skin appeared red and blotchy. Tossing from side to side, her fingers fluttered towards her throat, clearly in agitation. She was in a nightgown which allowed Josephine to examine her thoroughly, although there was very little need to do so given that it was more than apparent she had the very same fever that Josephine had been treating back in London.

"She has scarlet fever, Miss Peters," Josephine murmured, not turning her head. "I will use a mixture of vinegar and feverfew to bring down her temperature and she will have Doctor Thomas' medicine given to her regularly. In addition, I will make her broth and give it to her often in order to keep up her strength." A slight frown caught her brow. "How long has she been unwell, Miss Peters?" Doctor Thomas had stated that after the ninth day, patients had a much greater chance of improving and it was this that caught at Josephine's mind.

"Miss Peters?"

There came no response from the lady and, turning her head, Josephine saw with alarm that Miss Peters was now sitting in her chair with her head lolling back behind her.

"Miss Peters!"

Immediately, Josephine was by Miss Peters' side, her concern growing with every moment. The young lady had done a remarkable job to care for her mother alone but now it was obvious just how much of a toll it had taken on her. Pressing one hand gently to Miss Peters forehead, Josephine felt her heart plummet. Miss Peters was burning up.

"Miss Josephine, here are the things you require – oh!" Jones set down the tray by Lady Dunstable's bed before hurrying over to where Josephine stood by Miss Peters, his expression anxious.

"Is she unwell?"

"I think so," Josephine replied, grimly. "Jones, she will need to be taken to her bedchamber. And I will require another tray of precisely the same thing."

Jones nodded, looking a little concerned. "Of course, it is just that I do not think I can carry her alone."

Josephine moved towards Lady Dunstable, feeling a little overwhelmed. She now had not one noble lady under her care, but two. "I am sure Lord Dunstable will be able to help you, Jones. I must see to Lady Dunstable for the moment."

Jones muttered something under his breath and

looked at Miss Peters helplessly. Unable to do anything else, Josephine dabbed the cloth in water and ran it lightly over Lady Dunstable's forehead, waiting for Lord Dunstable to reappear with her belongings.

"Here you are, Miss Josephine."

She glanced up to see Lord Dunstable stop dead as he walked into the room, her cotton bag in his hand.

"Miss Peters is unwell," Jones murmured, as Lord Dunstable's face drained of color. "We are to take her to her bedchamber."

Lord Dunstable's gaze slowly traveled towards Josephine, who saw a slow-growing terror grow in his eyes. His mother was ill, and now so was his sister. The fear of losing them both was growing with every moment.

"The bag, my lord," she murmured, seeing him jump slightly before tentatively handing her the bag.

"What can I do?" he asked, hoarsely.

Josephine's heart clenched with sympathy. "Take your sister to her bedchamber," she replied, kindly. "I will come along to see her in a moment. Jones, might you ask the kitchen maid to make up some broth?"

The butler nodded. "Of course. Shall we, my lord?"

Under Josephine's watchful eye, Lord Dunstable and the butler took the limp form of Miss Peters out of the room, leaving her alone with Lady Dunstable.

Josephine quickly made up a mixture of water, vinegar and feverfew and placed a cloth within the bowl, letting it soak for a moment before wringing it out. Proceeding to gently dab at Lady Dunstable's face and neck, she saw the lady draw in a long breath, her eyelids fluttering for a moment.

CHAPTER 7

Lady Dunstable was terribly unwell.

The medicine Doctor Thomas had given her was quickly administered to the lady, with Josephine noting what time it had been given so that she could give the next dose in due course.

"Miss Josephine."

Lord Dunstable had returned, his face now a rather worrying shade of grey.

"What can I do now?"

"Sit."

Josephine indicated the tray by the fire, the tea cooling in the china cups.

"What do you mean?" Lord Dunstable asked, moving towards his mother. "There must be something more I can do."

Wringing out the cloth, Josephine set it gently on Lady Dunstable's forehead, pulling the bedcovers a little further down.

"She is a little more settled," Josephine murmured, looking up at Lord Dunstable. "Until the broth is made, there is little more I can do."

Lord Dunstable's eyes were fixed on his mother's flushed face.

"I have given her medicine and she is a little more at ease now, my lord," Josephine continued, trying to reassure him. "I will go and see to your sister now but you must sit and rest. Drink your tea and eat. Do send for me if there is any change."

She made to move to the door, only for Lord Dunstable to catch her arm.

"Sit for a moment, Miss Josephine," he murmured.

"You are pale and exhausted. The butler and the maid are still ensuring my sister is settled so you have a few minutes."

Josephine was about to refuse, only for her stomach to growl horribly. Doctor Thomas' words came back to her with force – *'you must not neglect yourself in order to tend to others'*. At the time, she had not understood it, only for Sam to explain to her that the doctor needed her to rest and to eat, simply to ensure that she did not fall into an exhaustion that would make her useless to everyone.

"For a few minutes," she said reluctantly, as Lord Dunstable still held her hand. "But then I must go to Miss Peters."

Lord Dunstable nodded and let her sit down before seating himself. Letting out a long breath, he ran one hand over his forehead, his gaze drifting back towards his mother before he remembered what he was meant to be doing. Pouring the tea for them both, he gestured to Josephine to help herself to the biscuits on the tray, which she did at once. She was hungry, she realized, eating it quickly and then reaching for another, and there would not be a lot of time to eat.

"There is nothing I can do?" Lord Dunstable asked, his eyes filled with worry. "I feel so useless here, sitting alone and watching over my mother."

Josephine reached across the table and took his hand. There was a solidarity growing between them already, even though they were only briefly acquainted. She knew precisely what he was feeling, having endured it already herself. Unfortunately, her hopes and her prayers had never come to anything, for both her parents had succumbed to the fever. She could not let him give up hope, she realized, seeing him look at her with desperation. Hope was the only thing he had at the moment.

"You must pray, my lord," she replied, in a compassionate voice. "Watch over your mother, watch over your sister and send your prayers to heaven that they might be spared."

Lord Dunstable shook his head. "I have never been much of a praying man."

"Then you must become one now," she replied, firmly, knowing that it would give him a purpose whilst she continued to treat Lady Dunstable and Miss Peters. "I know that you have a good deal to do in the estate at the moment and that in itself will be beneficial to us all." She smiled at him, her fingers tightening on his for a moment. "You are doing more than enough already, Lord Dunstable."

Slowly, his fingers twined with hers, his eyes glinting as a sense of purpose began to rest on his shoulders. "I understand, Miss Josephine. Of course, I will make sure to watch over my mother and my sister whenever I can. You must rest also, of course."

"We will support one another," she replied, aware of the warmth shooting up her arm from where their fingers touched. "Jones, the kitchen maid, and I are all here to help the Dunstable estate in whatever way we can."

He closed his eyes for a moment, his lips pulled tight as he drew in a steadying breath. "Thank you, Miss Josephine," he replied, his voice barely louder than a whisper. "You have given me a little hope and for that, I cannot thank you enough."

Her smile remained steady although her thoughts about what would happen with Lady Dunstable and Miss Peters were far from certain. "Thank you for trusting me, Lord Dunstable," she replied, gently. "I will not leave your side until this dark time is over."

CHAPTER EIGHT

Gideon felt sweat trickle down his back. The day had been long and he was tired. The horses were, at least, taken care of and were now all fed and watered, ready to rest and sleep.

His whole body was trembling slightly as he made his way towards the hen coop. He had not even realized they kept chickens, and Josephine had laughed as she'd pointed it out to him. To collect the eggs each day was not something he was used to but he did it regardless, even though he had no idea what to do with them after that.

Chucking out a handful of seeds to the hens – who all appeared to be delighted to see him – he quickly gathered the eggs and set them all down in the basket. The hens would put themselves into the coop and he'd have to go out later to shut it all up. The last thing they needed was a fox coming to take the chickens for themselves!

The old tree stump beside the coop called to him and, giving into his weakness, he sat down heavily. The hens ignored him, too busy looking for any stray bits of corn to come anywhere near him and Gideon felt himself glad for the few minutes of solitude.

His life had taken a very different turn this last week. He had done more than he'd ever done in his life before, waking up before dawn to go out to see the animals and bring in the milk that one of the kind village folk left for them just outside the servant's door. Thankfully, he didn't have to make breakfast since the kitchen maid, Gillian, managed to make enough for all of them. He and Miss Josephine usually ate together, with Josephine able to tell him how his mother, his sister, and the footmen had fared overnight.

She was exhausted, he could see that by the shadows under her eyes, the lines on her face, and yet she always had a smile for him, a quick flash of hope that kept him going.

After breakfast, they all worked together – himself, Miss Josephine and Jones – to clean and clear his mother's room and then his sister's. Miss Josephine and the kitchen maid would change the bedsheets and later, he'd find them both washing the old ones. He'd hated to see his mother and sister casting up their accounts but had stood by their side and held them up as they'd done so, the sight and smell turning his stomach. They'd all had to pull together as one. There was no job too beneath him, not even the emptying of the chamber pots.

Tiredness ran though him but he forced himself to stand. How Miss Josephine continued on and on, hour after hour, day after day, he did not know. She seemed so resilient, so determined, and thanks to her care, his

CHAPTER 8

mother and sister were not getting any worse. They both were given medicine every day, carefully bathed with vinegar and feverfew and had broth carefully spooned into their mouths. Their fevers, at least, had seemed to lessen and that was, no doubt, thanks to Miss Josephine's careful and steady attentions.

Running one hand through his hair, Gideon suddenly realized just how little he had thought of Georgina of late. He had written her a short note stating that his mother had become ill but, since then, he had not heard from her and nor had he written to her again. That in itself came as no surprise, since he had been so caught up with all that was going on, but to not think of her for a single moment? That took him a little by surprise. He had not been concerned for her welfare, had not wondered where she was at the present moment, had not so much as thought of whether she was still in London or now had returned to her father's home as she had planned. Georgina, for her part, had not written to him either, which suggested that she did not particularly care either. That brought no stab of pain to Gideon's heart. In fact, it did not give him more than a moment's pause, even though this was to be the woman he was to spend the rest of his days with. The woman who would bear his children, who would grow old with him.

That made him consider matters in a very different light. This terrible fever that had taken such a grip of his house now brought fresh matters into view, making Gideon realize that he would have to consider his future with Georgina with a great deal of seriousness. Could he really marry someone who cared so little for him, and for whom he did not give more than half a thought upon occasion? She was beautiful, yes, but he realized he knew very little about her. He did not know, nor did he care, about what she did with her time, what novels she enjoyed or what music she preferred. He did not know whether she enjoyed walking or riding the most. Surely one ought to know such things about one's betrothed?

The thought continued to gnaw at him as he made his way back towards the house, the basket of eggs in his hand. It was not as though he did not have enough on his mind already, but the sudden realization that he had not once thought of Georgina in this last week continued to plague him.

Walking in through the servant's entrance, he set down the eggs carefully before going to check on the two footmen who, thanks to Josephine's hard work and tender care now appeared to be doing a good deal better. Josephine had said she hoped they would make a full recovery and, as he stepped into the room to see them both eating broth of their own accord, a smile spread across his face.

"My lord," one of them said, still looking a little feverish but a good deal better none the less. "I think I should be able to get out of bed soon and help you, as I ought. I –"

Gideon held up a hand. "You are not to get out of your bed and resume your duties until Miss Josephine says that you are ready to do so," he replied, with a small smile. "You look a good deal better the both of you, and I am greatly relieved to see that."

CHAPTER 8

The second footman, Marks, smiled with relief. "I am glad of it too, my lord."

"It is very good to see your strength returning," Gideon said, feeling his stomach grumble slightly at the sight and smell of the broth the two footmen had. "If you should need anything, you need but ring for Jones or Miss Josephine – or myself, if they are busy."

The two footmen nodded and gave him their thanks and Gideon excused himself, feeling his hunger growing all the more.

There was plenty of broth but Gideon had to admit that he was growing a little tired of eating the same thing every day. Making his way to the pantry, he began to look through the shelves but found himself growing angry, realizing that he had very little idea what to do with any of it. For heaven's sake, he did not even know how to make a loaf of bread! It was either Gillian, the kitchen maid, or Miss Josephine who baked one every morning. Normally, Gillian would have been able to make something more than just broth and bread for dinner but his mother had required a little more attention of late, which he did not know was either a good thing or a bad. Either way, she was not present and able to make him anything, which meant he was entirely on his own.

Something moved in the bag of flour he was looking at, making him jump with fright. Staggering back, he felt his breath catch in his chest in disgust, realizing that there were insects of some kind in the flour. Insects! That flour could not be used, surely!

"And just how many more are there within these walls?" he muttered to himself, his eyes going from one sack of flour to another, feeling his stomach churn. He had been working so hard and now all of the food in the pantry might well be contaminated by all kinds of creatures! Running his hands through his hair, Gideon let out a long, heavy sigh. He had no idea where to go to fetch more flour and, even if he did have clean flour, he could not make something out of it. Aside from looking after the animals and managing to sweep a floor or two, he was next to useless.

His stomach growled louder and, muttering darkly under his breath, Gideon stomped out of the pantry – only to walk straight into Miss Josephine.

"Oh!"

Catching her arms, Gideon made to steady Miss Josephine as she staggered back, his hands tight as he held her steadily.

"Goodness, Lord Dunstable, I did not see you there," Miss Josephine said, with a small smile. "Are you quite all right? Whatever were you doing in the pantry?"

Slowly, he let her go, his arms falling to his sides as frustration and disappointment ran through him. "I thought to find something to eat," he replied, with a shrug of his shoulders. "But it is next to useless. There are insects of some kinds in the flour and besides which, I – I do not have any skill with such matters."

He let his gaze slip from Miss Josephine, afraid that she would laugh at him but, to his surprise, she stepped forward and looked over his shoulder into the pantry.

"Show me."

Looking at her, he saw her eyes warm as she smiled at him – and something began to curl in his belly.

CHAPTER 8

"Show me the insects," she insisted, taking his hand when he did not immediately move. "If they're what I think they are, then there is no reason that we cannot use the flour as it is."

"As it is?" he repeated, astonished enough by her reaction to move into the pantry with her. "We cannot use flour that has those things in it, surely?"

Miss Josephine let out a laugh as he pointed to the sack of flour. "My dear sir, you have very little understanding of what life is like for those beneath your station. When I lived with my parents, we often found these weevils in our flour." She tipped her head and smiled at him. "My mother sieved them out as best she could and then used the flour regardless – just as we will do now."

This made him pause, a realization of just how different their lives were beginning to sweep over him. "I see. You are quite right, Miss Josephine. I do not understand such a way of living."

"That is not your fault," she replied, gently, putting one hand on his arm. "I did not intend to shame you. It is just that your reaction to something such as this did make me laugh."

He could not help but smile despite the heat in his face. "I understand," he replied, gently. "Thank you, Miss Josephine."

She dropped her hand and, for a moment, the air crackled between them. They were in such a small space, almost pressed together as their eyes met, his gaze holding hers.

And then, Miss Josephine cleared her throat.

"Might you take this sack out to the kitchen?" she

asked, stepping past him. "I will find the sieve and we will make ourselves a pie or two."

His stomach growled loudly and, to his embarrassment, Miss Josephine heard it, throwing her head back in laughter. Gideon, despite his red face, found himself joining in the laughter, the mirth lifting his spirits.

"I can tell you are hungry, Lord Dunstable," Miss Josephine chuckled, as he set the flour on the worn kitchen table. "Should you be able to help me, then I think we could make a couple of meat pies and perhaps an apple pie or two for dessert? Would that satisfy your hunger pangs?"

Smiling at her, Gideon spread his hands. "If you are not too exhausted, Miss Josephine. I would not like you to weary yourself even more than you have been doing."

"Well, Lord Dunstable, the very reason I came to find you was to inform you that I believe your mother has greatly improved today," Miss Josephine replied, setting down the sieve onto the table before going in search of a bowl. "That is why Gillian has been with her for so long. Lady Dunstable has been hungry today, which is a very good sign. Gillian has been giving her broth and bread, as well as water whenever she is thirsty. She is not yet able to rise from her bed but I hope she will be able to sit up tomorrow. I know she will be glad to see you."

Gideon felt his breath sucked from his body, forced to lean on the table in front of him for a moment. His mother was not going to die, it seemed. The fever had not taken her. She was recovering.

"And your sister is not as sick as your mother was, I do not think," Miss Josephine continued, her voice gentling as she saw his expression. "I feel sure she will recover also. Doctor Thomas always said that after nine days, the patient is more than likely to make an improvement. Miss Peters is strong. She will do that, my lord, I am certain of it."

His breath shuddered out of him, his entire body trembling violently for a moment. This was more than he had expected, more than he could almost take in. He was not going to be left alone. He would have his sister and his mother back again, in time.

"Thank you, Miss Josephine," he breathed, his voice breaking with emotion. "I cannot share with you just how much gratitude I have for what you have done." Tears sprang to his eyes and he blinked them away rapidly, his gaze dropping to the table as he dragged air into his lungs.

Something warm touched his hand and he twisted his head to look at her, seeing Miss Josephine's gentle expression. She was standing so close to him, trying to comfort him as best she could and his appreciation grew all the more.

"Thank you, Miss Josephine," he said again, his voice barely more than a whisper. "Thank you."

"You have done your part too, my lord," she replied, as her fingers twined with his. "Your mother has recovered, thanks to you and to Jones also. She will require you to be by her side all the more these next few days. Which is why," she continued, a little more briskly, "we must make these pies. Lady Dunstable will need to eat something a little more substantial in the coming days. Gillian did say that there was meat in the pantry, in the cool box."

Gideon reluctantly let go of her hand, looking at her with such admiration that he could feel it warm all through him. Here was a lady with more fortitude, more strength and more determination than he himself possessed. She had fought on with an almost relentless spirit, doing all she could to keep his mother and sister battling against the fever, whilst still somehow managing to cook, clean and generally aid him in his running of the house.

Without being aware that he was even doing it, he pulled Miss Josephine into his arms and held her tightly, feeling his breathing growing ragged as he battled the tears that came to his eyes once again.

He tried to thank her but nothing came from his lips other than a harsh sigh. Miss Josephine seemed to understand, however, for her arms wrapped about his waist, her head resting gently against his chest.

When she tipped her head up to look at him, a gentle smile on her face, he could not help but lean down and press his lips to her cheek. How had he ever been so blessed as to have such a wonderful creature stumble into his path? Had he not ended up at the Devil's basement, then he might never have found her, might never have known the relief that came with his mother and sister's recovery. Raising his head, he heard her breath catch and, for a moment, an entirely different emotion ran through him.

Their eyes locked as he saw her cheeks color, surprised that he found himself thinking that, despite the tiredness in her eyes, she was rather pretty. Dismissing the thought, he smiled at her and saw her tentatively smile back, the blush darkening her cheeks all the more.

"You are going to be quite all right, Lord Dunstable," she whispered, as he slowly, reluctantly let her go. "Everything is going to be just as it once was. All it needs is a little more time."

"A little more time," he murmured, suddenly realizing that one day soon, Miss Josephine would no longer be in his life and finding his heart dropping to the floor at the thought. "You will stay until you are certain they are both truly recovered?"

Her smile broadened. "But of course, my lord," she replied, moving back towards the weevil-infested flour. "You have my word."

It was all he needed.

CHAPTER NINE

"And how are you today, Lady Dunstable?"

The lady smiled back at Josephine and Josephine noticed that there was a little color in her cheeks this morning. It had been five days since she had first told Lord Dunstable that she believed his mother was on the way to a full recovery and since then, not only had Lady Dunstable improved but his sister, Miss Peters, had begun to recover also. The footmen below stairs continued to improve, to the point that one of them was already out of bed and attempting to help where he could, despite Josephine's warnings to take his time and not put himself under any additional strain.

"I feel a good deal more like myself, Josephine," Lady Dunstable said, resting her head back against the pillows. "Might I get up this morning? Even for a short time?"

Josephine hesitated for a moment but nodded. She did not know how to deal with a lady of quality wanting to rise from her bed, having only the experience of the poor and needy in the Devil's basement back in Smithfield Market. Once they had been able enough to rise, Doctor Thomas had sent them back to their home – if they still had one – to be cared for by relatives, if they still had any. Otherwise, they were sent to one of the recovery wards, which had been set up all around London for those who had nowhere else to go but had managed to survive the fever.

"So long as you have Gillian with you," she said, slowly. "And so long as you return to your bed the moment you begin to feel tired. The fever will have taken your strength and you will need to build it up slowly."

Lady Dunstable beamed with delight at this news and Josephine felt glad for such a biddable patient. Had she told Lady Dunstable that she ought to remain abed for another day or so, Josephine knew that she would not have complained.

"I had best to see Miss Peters." Josephine rose to her feet, just as Lord Dunstable came in. "Do excuse me."

"But of course," Lady Dunstable smiled, as Lord Dunstable came to sit by her side. "Thank you, Josephine."

Josephine caught Lord Dunstable's eye for a moment and saw him smile at her, his gaze lingering for an overly long moment. Her heart quickened but she turned her head away, berating herself for such foolishness. Lord Dunstable was a baron and she nothing more than a maid, if that. Whilst it was true that they had grown close over these last, difficult days, there was nothing more to it than that. She ought not to let her heart fill with thoughts of him, not when she was to leave this house very soon.

"Miss Peters," she said, forcing herself to think only of her patient. "I am glad to see you sitting up this morning. How do you feel?"

Miss Peters smiled wanly, as Gillian set aside the broth she had been feeding the lady.

"I am a little better, I think," Miss Peters replied, weakly. "Although I am very tired."

Josephine smiled gently and came to sit on the edge of the bed. "That is to be expected, Miss Peters. I –"

"Francine, please," Miss Peters interrupted, putting one hand over Josephine's. "You have done so much for me that I cannot allow you to remain so proper in your address. Please, Josephine."

Josephine smiled happily, recalling just how upset Miss Peters had been at her arrival and finding herself grateful that Miss Peters' opinion of her had changed so drastically. "Thank you, Francine," she replied, pleasantly. "As I was saying, you have battled scarlet fever for some days and now, I'm afraid, it will take time for you to recover entirely. Your skin will need to be bathed and it may peel." She saw Francine frown and felt herself grow all the more sympathetic. "I will do all I can for you to soften the discomfort," she promised. "Your throat still aches, does it?"

Francine nodded. "A little, but it does not burn as it once did."

Satisfied to hear this, Josephine let out a long breath of relief. "I am very glad to hear you say so, Francine. You are well on the way to recovery and, given that myself and Jones have not caught the fever, I would suggest that you need not fear catching it again. It seems as though having it once prevents you from having to endure it again."

"That is a small mercy," Francine replied, attempting to push herself up a little more. "And how is Mama?"

"Much better," Josephine replied, firmly. "She will want to see you, I am sure. Perhaps tomorrow she will have enough strength to come to your room."

Francine nodded and smiled, a single tear trickling down her cheek. "I am so glad. Thank you, Josephine."

"I did not do it all," Josephine said gently. "Your brother has worked tirelessly, as have Jones and Gillian. Everyone has been doing their utmost to ensure you and Lady Dunstable have recovered."

There was a moment of silence as Josephine held Francine's gaze.

"And yet, I think we have you to thank the most, Josephine."

She turned her head and caught Lord Dunstable's eye, her stomach tightening as he came closer. She could not look away, seeing the warmth in his eyes and finding herself unable to turn away. He put one hand on her shoulder and her heart slammed against her chest, her breathing quickening just a little.

"You are a marvel, my dear Josephine," he said, with such tenderness that Josephine felt her face flush with heat. "You have brought my sister and my mother through the most terrible of illnesses. In time, I believe our home will return to how it once was."

"You mean to call the servants back?" Francine asked, breaking the moment that had been steadily growing between Josephine and Lord Dunstable.

"In a day or so," Lord Dunstable replied, his gaze lifting from Josephine and allowing her to breathe a little easier. "Once you are both stronger. We appear to be managing quite well, it seems." His hand rose from Josephine's shoulder and she stood at once, thinking to leave Lord Dunstable and his sister alone.

"I should return to the kitchens to prepare something to eat," she said, seeing Francine's eyes grow heavy. "Gillian, might you go to Lady Dunstable's side? She wishes to sit in her seat by the fire."

"There is no need," Lord Dunstable said, easily. "I have helped her to her chair and she is enjoying tea and a few small biscuits I managed to unearth in the kitchen."

Josephine saw Gillian nod, her eyes drifting back to where Francine began to rest heavily against the pillows.

"Mayhap you would be best remaining here, Gillian," Lord Dunstable suggested tenderly, seeing his sister falling asleep. "I will help you, Josephine, with whatever it is you need to do."

She lifted one brow, trying to push away the feelings of affection that had begun to trouble her so much of late. "I need to cook and bake, my lord. Are you truly willing to attempt such a thing again?" She saw the corner of his mouth tip upwards, recalling how ineffective he had been in his efforts to help her bake a meat pie and apple pie some days ago.

"I can wash the utensils and the like," he suggested, offering her his arm as though she was a rich lady whom he was taking for a short stroll. "Or I can make some tea. I am sure Gillian would like some, if you do not?"

The maid blushed and nodded and Josephine, having

no other recourse but to accept his arm, did so at once. Lord Dunstable led her from the room, chatting amicably all the way as they made their way down the servant's staircase.

"I do not think I shall ever take my staff for granted again," he said, as they reached the kitchens. "Gillian, Jones and the footmen who have remained will all have a decent increase in their wages, I think. In fact, I may raise all of their salaries, but give Gillian and Jones a little more for their devotion and dedication."

She smiled, finding him to be a most generous man. "I know that would be greatly appreciated, my lord."

Lord Dunstable made to say more but was interrupted by the butler, who appeared out of nowhere to hand him a letter. He then took the tea tray Josephine had been preparing with the promise to take it to Gillian. Josephine could see the weariness on his face and pressed him to remain with her and take a few moments of rest, adding another teacup to the tray. Lord Dunstable muttered something under his breath, his eyes on the letter, and Jones melted away at once, leaving Josephine feeling a little ill at ease.

"I will leave you, my lord," she murmured, making for the door of the kitchen. "You will want to read this alone, of course."

His head shot up, his eyes fixed on her. "No," he replied, with a good deal more firmness than she had expected. "No, indeed, Josephine. You are to stay. It is only a letter from a friend."

Breaking the seal, Lord Dunstable unfolded the letter and began to read, leaving Josephine feeling as though she were intruding, even though he had insisted she remain. Forcing her attention to the task at hand, she found all she would need to make yet more apple pies, knowing that Lady Dunstable and Miss Peters would enjoy the sweetness. Lord Dunstable would need something to eat for dinner too, of course, along with the rest of them, which meant she would have to get Gillian to help her make some kind of stew with whatever they had left in the pantry. Josephine was glad that she would soon be receiving a little more help in the form of the footmen, since they were both now recovering. The rest of the servants would be able to return soon, just as long as the fever did not touch anyone else. Silently, she sent up a prayer of thanks that she had been protected from the fever, although her heart still mourned the loss of her parents. A small smile touched her lips as she realized just how much of a healing had taken place in her own heart whilst she had been working here at the Dunstable estate. Lord Dunstable had done more than he knew, in working alongside her. There was a friendship, a kinship, growing between them and it was this that brought a joy to Josephine's heart.

"I should have expected nothing less."

Her eyes darted to Lord Dunstable as he scrunched up the letter in his hand, before slamming it down hard on the kitchen table. She jumped with surprise and looked away, her cheeks darkening red as she tried not to look at him. Whatever had been in that letter, it was obvious Lord Dunstable was not particularly happy about the contents.

"Foolish woman!" Lord Dunstable muttered, darkly,

sweeping one hand through his hair before leaning both hands on the table, his head drawing low as he drew in a breath. "There is no good reason why –"

Josephine cleared her throat gently, wanting to remind him that she was still present in the room. It was obvious that Lord Dunstable was deeply troubled by his letter but she did not want him to say more than he ought in front of her.

"My apologies, Josephine," he said, after a moment. "I am just a little upset."

She arched one eyebrow. "I can see that, my lord," she replied, with a small smile. "The sole reason for my interruption was simply to remind you of my presence here, when it is obviously a very private matter."

He snorted. "It is not of a particularly private nature," he muttered, standing up and looking down at the crumpled up note that now lay on the table. "There is a friend of the family that shows no concern for my mother or my sister and that troubles me greatly. To have someone I thought at least cared a little for those I hold dear write to me in such a fashion has deeply upset me."

She held his gaze for a moment, seeing the lines of fatigue and frustration on his face. "I am sorry, my lord."

He did not look away, his expression growing all the more intense as they stood together in the kitchens. "You need not apologize, Josephine," he rumbled, moving a little closer to her. "You show more compassion to my mother and sister than those I would have considered to be my friends. You have toiled in your efforts to bring them back to full health and strength, giving up so much of yourself in order to do so. You cannot know just how much I admire you."

Her heart leaped in her chest. Admiration? This was not something she had expected to hear from the baron, not when she was nothing more than a street beggar!

"You are quite remarkable, Josephine," Lord Dunstable continued, putting one hand on her shoulder in what she thought to be a gesture of support. Her heart began to hammer violently until she was sure Lord Dunstable would be able to hear it.

"I do not think I will ever be able to find another living soul with such heart, such compassion, such tenderness, and such strength," Lord Dunstable finished, his blue eyes darkening just a touch as he looked down at her. "I do not think I can let you return to London, Josephine. Not yet."

She licked her lips, suddenly nervous, finding herself moving a little closer to him as though to encourage his nearness. She did not know what it was he meant and certainly didn't have the courage to ask him. He was standing so close to her now, standing with such a deep intensity in his gaze that she found herself almost burning with a fierce and unexpected heat. Her whole body was frozen in place, her apple pies forgotten as she looked up at him.

"Lord Dunstable!"

The sound of the butler's voice seemed to jolt Lord Dunstable back to the present and Josephine felt his hand lift from her shoulder, sending an unwelcome chill all through her.

"Lord Dunstable, some of the staff have returned!"

CHAPTER 9

Jones exclaimed, his eyes bright as he looked from Lord Dunstable to Josephine and back again. "We have three maids and the cook, as well as the groom, the stable boys, and two more footmen. They are all standing outside, waiting to hear whether or not they can return to the house, my lord. The news of Lady Dunstable and Miss Peters recovery must have spread!"

Lord Dunstable's face lit up with delight, his eyes widening just a little as he looked back at his ever-faithful butler. "Returned, you say?" he said, walking towards the servant's entrance. "Then come, Jones. Let us greet them all and welcome them back to the estate. Their presence here will be most welcome!"

Josephine watched him go, her eyes unable to lift themselves from his form until he walked out of sight. Confusion and nervous anticipation ran through her. She did not know what it was Lord Dunstable had intended to do – if anything – but the way she felt about him was no longer able to be hidden. Her heart was flickering with affection and longing, which she both hated and accepted. To care for the lord of the house was ridiculous indeed but regardless of that, there was a hope lingering in her heart. He had not stepped away when their gazes had locked, he had not taken a step back when she had moved a little closer. Instead, he had seemed to welcome it. What did that mean? What *could* it mean? Or was she letting her foolish heart fill with dreams that would never come to anything?

CHAPTER TEN

Three days later and Gideon felt as though everything was slowly returning back to normal. His mother was now able to come down to the drawing room for a short part of the day and his sister, now free of the fever entirely, was able to sit by the fire in her room. Josephine had promised her that she could come down to the drawing-room herself tomorrow, once she had garnered a little more strength.

He rubbed the velvety nose of his stallion, Hunter, and smiled to himself. Josephine was the best of women, for she had worked tirelessly and unendingly in an attempt to bring about this now happy situation. He could not thank her enough for what she had done, finding his thoughts almost always turning towards her. They had grown rather close these last two weeks and he found his heart a little painful at the thought of her returning to London.

A sudden weakness rushed through him and he was

forced to hold onto the stable door for a moment, his eyes closing tightly. Evidently, he was not the only one who required a little more rest.

"Are you all right, my lord?"

He opened his eyes to see one of the stable hands looking at him with concern, although Gideon noticed that the man kept his distance.

"I am quite well," he said, firmly. "Might you saddle Hunter? I thought to take a short ride this afternoon."

Hunter, as though understanding what was said, tossed his mane and whinnied loudly, making Gideon laugh.

"Of course, my lord," the stable hand chuckled, going in search of a saddle. "If you'll just give me a minute or two."

Gideon nodded. "Of course." Making his way outside into the weak afternoon sunshine, he leaned back against the stable wall and let out a long breath. The letter Georgina had written him was still lingering in his thoughts, even though he had done his best to push them aside. Georgina, so foolish and so selfish, had struck his heart another blow, to the point that he was now considering their future together with great solemnity.

The truth was, he did not want to marry Georgina. She was vapid and disinteresting, caring only for how she looked and what gowns she wore. The way that she had turned her back on not only himself but on his mother and sister had torn at his heart, for she had not so much as expressed even a single hint of interest in how his family fared.

When he had written to her to inform her that the

sickness was leaving his house and that the servants had returned, he had received nothing more than a short, rather curt, reply. She was still in London, it seemed, keeping away from all those who were ill with the fever. For whatever reason, her father had not yet sent her the carriage – which, Gideon considered, might have been because her father had not yet returned home. Thinking that his daughter was safe with Gideon, he might have lingered a while on his return to his country seat. There were plenty of inns and the like, which could entertain a gentleman for some days if he so wished. Regardless, Georgina was still in London and yet, despite the fever raging in the streets, she did not wish to see him. Rather unkindly, she had stated that even if there was a hint of fever in his household, she would not venture anywhere near. There had not been any exultations of delight over his mother and sister's recovery, had not so much as mentioned how glad she was that Josephine had been able to bring about such a strong recovery. No, all Georgina cared about was her own safety and her own health. She had not even asked after his own health, had not once considered to see how he fared in all of this! Compared to Josephine, who so often sought him out simply to ask how he was feeling so that she might assist him in any way she could, Georgina's selfishness burned brightly.

It burned away his thoughts of marrying her, realizing that he could not do so now. Not when it was so clear that she felt very little for him, and he felt nothing for her. Gideon knew it had been the express wish of his father that he marry Georgina, but in this, he would have to fail in his duty. He could not wed someone so cold, so uncaring. To be bound to her for life would be nothing more than torturous. Even the thought of bringing children into such a union sent a cold shiver down his spine, for he did not think that Georgina would be a caring mother.

Josephine, however.....

His eyes shot open. Josephine? Was he truly considering having Josephine as his wife, when she was nothing more than a woman taken from the London streets?

Why should that matter?

The quiet voice niggled at him, forcing him to question everything he knew, everything he had once believed about marriage and suitability. Josephine did not come from a noble background or good family, and certainly did not have any sort of dowry to come with her – but she was good and kind, caring and loving, strong and determined. She gave of herself until there was almost nothing left, working hard and striving continuously for others. Did it matter who her family had been? Did it matter to his heart whether or not she was gentry?

Gideon closed his eyes again, a long breath escaping him. No, it ought not to matter. It ought not to send him into such a dizzying conflict to admit that he found his heart considering the lady more and more each day and yet the struggle still remained.

Josephine was not of his class, not of his ilk, and that expectation still weighed heavily on his shoulders. He was a baron, with responsibilities of all sorts, and Josephine would not know or understand what such a life was like. That being said, she did speak wonderfully well, thanks to the housekeeper who had taken such an interest in her. He could not fault her in that but still, there were so many other things that she would need to learn.

"But could you not teach her?" he muttered aloud, as if trying to convince himself. "Could you not show her, just as she has shown you so many things?"

His lips slowly began to curve into a smile, his body relaxing slowly against the stable wall. Yes, he could teach her what a life here was like. Yes, he could show her the responsibilities expected of a baron, just as she had taught him how to cook a simple meal, or how to mix up the medicine required for his mother and sister. She had taught him so much already and he had taken her tuition eagerly. Mayhap it was time for her to learn something new also.

"Class be damned," he said aloud, pushing himself up from the stable wall. He would not allow his accident of birth to set them both apart. One could not choose where one was born. He was a baron, and she the daughter of a laborer, with no-one else left in the world, and yet Gideon knew he could not be parted from her. He could not let her disappear into the ether never to be a part of his life again. Such a thought brought him a searing pain in his heart, a pain he did not ever want to truly experience. Josephine was in his heart now and he did not think that she would ever truly leave it.

"Here you are, my lord."

Gideon made to stand away from the wall, only for a rush of heat to pour over him, forcing him to stagger back, one hand over his eyes. The stable hand grasped his arm, supporting him for a moment until the heat dissipated from Gideon's bones.

"I am quite all right," Gideon muttered, not quite sure what had just occurred. "I think it must be the exhaustion of the last few days creeping up on me."

The stable hand nodded, looking a little concerned. "If you are quite sure, my lord."

"Quite," Gideon replied, feeling much more like himself again. "Thank you." He mounted Hunter easily, strength returning to him. "I'll be an hour or so, I should think."

The stable hand nodded and Gideon pushed Hunter into a fast trot, letting the cool air brush over his face as he rode. His breath caught as he saw Josephine wander along one of the many paths that led through the estate gardens, seeing her idly letting her hand trail through some long grasses. Even if he had tried, Gideon knew he could not keep away from her.

"Josephine!"

Turning at once, her eyes registered surprise for a moment before a welcoming smile tugged at her lips. Gideon found himself smiling back, his heart quickening just a little.

"Good afternoon, my lord," Josephine smiled, as he jumped down from his horse to stand beside her. "A fine afternoon for a ride, it seems!"

He chuckled. "Indeed. I confess I have missed riding these last weeks." Tipping his head, he looked at her for a moment. "Do you enjoy such things?"

She laughed, although her cheeks darkened with color. "My lord, you forget. I am nothing more than a lowly maid and the daughter of a laborer. I confess that riding a horse is not something I have often been used to."

An idea caught at his mind. "Then should you like me to show you?"

Her eyes widened for a moment. "My lord, I do not think..."

"Come here," he chuckled, grasping her lightly around the waist and leading her towards Hunter, who was happily munching the lush green grass of his lawn which, of late, had not been as well maintained. His body grew warm with the closeness of her, seeing her flushed cheeks and hearing the quickening of her breath. When she glanced up at him, he felt his own breath catch in his chest, finding himself captivated by her green eyes. She was beautiful, in both face and in character, and he could not help but be drawn to her.

"Let me help you, Josephine," he murmured, as they drew near to the horse. "Do not be afraid."

Her hands rested on his forearms. "I am not afraid," she replied, her voice a little higher than before, making him chuckle. "But you will lead him, won't you?" She eyed Hunter a little suspiciously, taking in his large size.

"Of course I will," he promised, holding her about the waist with two hands for a moment, before lifting her up into the saddle.

Josephine let out a small shriek, before grasping onto the pommel with both hands.

"You are not going to fall," he assured her, a smile spreading across his face as she let out a long breath, steadying herself. "Hunter is an easy horse, despite his stature. Come, let us walk towards the lake."

Josephine gave a jerky nod, her eyes fixed on his face. "Just so long as you go slowly," she said quietly, her fingers white on the saddle.

He chuckled. "I will," he promised. "But by the time we reach there, I am quite sure you will be much more at ease."

The lake was beautiful today. The sunshine, though it was dim, bounced off the water, seeming to sparkle as they approached. Josephine was no longer desperately clinging to the pommel but had let go and was now loosely holding the reins, sitting up a little straighter. It made him glad to see it, smiling at her as she let out a small sigh of contentment.

"You see?" he said, as they came closer to the water. "You have the ability to ride, Josephine. You just need a little more practice."

She smiled at him as he held out his arms to her, ready to help her down. Hunter was already busy eating the grass, clearly ignoring the two of them as he ate. Josephine twisted her body a little and leaned down into him, only to let out a small cry as she half-fell out of the saddle.

"I have you!" he laughed, catching her carefully and setting her down. "That is one thing about Hunter I will say – he can appear to be rather high off the ground!"

Josephine did not laugh but rested her head on his chest for a moment, her feet only just touching the ground. "Goodness," she breathed. "I think if I was ever to ride myself, I would need a much smaller horse."

"That is true," Gideon admitted, his mind suddenly full of the idea. If Josephine were to remain here with him, then he could help her choose her own mare, making sure to find one that was gentle enough for her to learn to ride. "I think, mayhap, Josephine, that is a very good idea."

Slowly, her head rose and her eyes met his. Confusion filled her expression as he let his fingers brush down her cheek, astonished by just how much he felt by a simple touch.

"Lord Dunstable," Josephine murmured, her cheeks dusting with pink. "I –"

"Dunstable, please," he interrupted, hating the formality. "We are beyond propriety I think, Josephine." His throat began to ache and he cleared it, grimacing as he did so. He had not expected such a close interaction with Josephine to bring him such sensations.

Josephine frowned. "Dunstable, are you quite well?"

He smiled. "More than well," he stated, firmly. "I have considered a good many things of late, Josephine and the truth is that I do not wish you to go from my life. I cannot bear the thought of you returning to London."

Her eyes widened, her mouth opened but she said nothing.

"I – I confess that these feelings are rather new to me," he stammered, feeling himself a little embarrassed. "I do not quite know what to do or say to you but one thing I do know.....I do not want you to leave."

Her cheeks darkened all the more. "I will not stay to be your – your –" Looking away, he saw her eyes spark with a faint glitter of anger and realized what she thought he meant.

"No, Josephine," he said firmly, catching a hold of her chin and looking deeply into her eyes. "Never as that. *Never* as that. I would not ask you to be my mistress, Josephine. I hold you in much too high a regard."

As he spoke, he saw her whole body relax, her anger fading away to be replaced with something like astonishment. Gideon realized that she had not stepped away from him, that she had not immediately rejected the proposition, feeling his heart rise with gladness that she was, in fact, still in his arms. Slowly, so slowly, her hands lifted to his chest, resting there with a tentativeness that had him drawing in a shaking breath. There was so much vulnerability, so much uncertainty and yet nothing changed what he felt in his heart.

"Josephine, I...." Another wave of weakness ran through him and he closed his eyes, unable to finish the sentence.

"Dunstable?" Josephine said, her hands now on his shoulders as her voice rang with concern.

He shook it away. "I am quite all right," he said, with a good deal less firmness than he had intended. "Truly, I am. This is all just a little overwhelming." Opening his eyes, he looked down at her, his eyes flickering to her lips. The urge to kiss her was growing steadily with every moment that passed, the awareness that they were quite alone only adding to that.

What about Georgina?

A wave of guilt rushed over him. He had decided not to marry Georgina, yes, but he had not, as yet, spoken to her about the matter. He had not told her that their engagement was at an end and yet here he was with another lady in his arms. That was not right. He ought to speak to Georgina first before he allowed himself to confess his feelings to Josephine. There was a responsibility still towards Georgina and as much as he wanted to lower his head and kiss Josephine with all the deep affection he felt, Gideon knew he could not.

"Perhaps we should return to the house," he said thickly, letting his hands drop to his sides. "I should not like anyone to question your integrity, Josephine – nor mine, for that matter."

She frowned, stepping away from him. "I don't understand, Dunstable."

He tried to explain without mentioning Georgina, his guilt turning to shame. "I should not like to have the servants questioning your reputation, Josephine," he stammered, trying to find some kind of excuse for his sudden coolness. "There are things I must make sense of, things I must first understand before I can give you all of myself."

Her eyes watched him with an intensity that felt as though his chest had been ripped open and his heart tugged apart for her to scrutinize. His breathing quickened and he rubbed his forehead with the back of his hand, feeling the sweat beading there. Suddenly, he felt rather ill.

"Josephine, I –"

Stumbling, he tried to move towards her but found his legs wobbling. She gasped and darted forward, catching him in her arms and supporting him with every bit of strength she had.

"You are unwell, Dunstable," Josephine gasped, holding him upright as she tried to help him move towards Hunter. "We must get back to the house. Can you pull yourself up onto Hunter?"

His vision was blurring as he looked at his horse, a little unsure how he was meant to climb up onto such a great height. His whole body was tired, weakness tugging at him as he put one foot wearily into the stirrup.

How he managed to get up onto the saddle, Gideon could not be sure. His head was growing painful, his throat aching as Josephine picked up the reins and, casting him a worried glance, began to walk hastily back towards the house. Hunter seemed to understand the urgency, breaking into a trot as they neared the stables.

"Hold on, my lord," he heard Josephine say, as the stable hand came out to greet them both. "We will have you in bed and resting very soon. You need not worry. I will look after you."

His voice was thick, his words rasping from a suddenly painful throat. "Josephine," he said, somehow finding himself on the ground, supported by the stable hand and a groomsman who had appeared from nowhere.

She took his hand for a moment, her smile a little uncertain. "I will take care of you, my lord," she promised, as they moved towards the house. "Do not fear. You will recover from the fever soon."

"The fever," he muttered, thickly. "So that's what it is. I have the fever."

Then everything went dark.

CHAPTER ELEVEN

"How does he fare?"

Josephine looked up to see Francine walk into the bedchamber, her eyes wide with concern.

"I'm afraid he has the fever," Josephine replied, gently. "But we have begun to treat him almost immediately, which I am sure is going to help." She swallowed her own fear, suddenly terrified that she would lose Lord Dunstable to the fever, just as she had lost her own mother and father. Everyone who mattered to her had already been taken, and now, just as she and Lord Dunstable had been on the verge of something inexplicably wonderful, he had been struck down by the fever. Turning back to Lord Dunstable, she saw him toss his head from one side to the other, clearly struggling with the fever already.

"Here," she said to Gillian, handing her the cool cloth so that she could dab at Lord Dunstable's forehead whilst she herself continued to mix up a fresh batch of vinegar and feverfew. Rising to her feet, she took Francine's hands in her own and tried to put as much certainty into her expression as she could.

"Your brother is strong," she said, in a calm, firm voice. "He will battle through this, I am quite sure of it. It may take some days but I will do all I can for him. I swear to you I will not leave his side."

Francine nodded tightly, her expression growing troubled. "And what if he does not recover?" she whispered, her fingers tightening on Josephine's. "What do we do then? The title will go to –"

"You need not think in such a way," Josephine interrupted, firmly. "Do not let fear take hold of your heart and mind, Francine. Trust that your brother will have the strength to pull through this terrible sickness. You and your mother have the same spirit and you have both recovered." She managed a small smile, seeing Francine's eyes fill with tears. "You must rest also. Your strength is not what it once was as yet."

Francine nodded. "I will help you whenever I can," she said, hoarsely. "I suppose I must write to Georgina. Last Dunstable said, she was still in London."

Josephine frowned, unsure as to who Francine was referring to. "Georgina?" she aside, letting go of Francine's hands in order to make up her mixture of feverfew and vinegar.

Francine nodded, moving to her brother's side and taking his hand. "Miss Georgina Wells, my brother's betrothed."

Josephine's hands stilled, her heart suddenly beating violently in her chest. Lord Dunstable was engaged?

"She was here for a very short time," Francine continued, clearly unaware of the devastation her words were causing to Josephine. "But the moment she knew the servants were unwell, she left this place and returned to London in order to return with her father to his country seat. From what Dunstable said, Georgina's father, Viscount Armitage, had already begun his journey back to the country and had not yet sent his carriage for her." She shook her head, shooting a glance towards Josephine who felt as though she were frozen in place, confusion and upset mounting with every moment. "The foolish girl thought it best to remain in London, where the fever rages, rather than return here to aid us. I know Dunstable was terribly upset over her recent letter to him, but regardless of that, I should still inform her of his condition."

"Of course," Josephine replied, woodenly, recalling just how upset Lord Dunstable had been some days ago, when he had read a letter in the kitchen and then crumpled it up in his hand. She did not know at the time why he had been so upset but now realized that this letter must have been from his betrothed, Miss Georgina Wells. Daughter of a viscount, part of the nobility and certainly a good deal more suitable for a baron than the likes of her.

And yet, Lord Dunstable had drawn near to her upon receiving the letter, hadn't he? He had been upset that his betrothed showed him no concern, showed no consideration for the illness of his mother and sister and then, subsequently, had stepped closer to her. The air had grown thick between them and she had felt her heart beating with a frantic hope, only for Jones the butler to interrupt them. Even this afternoon, Lord Dunstable had spoken to her with such truth in his eyes that she had struggled to accept what he had said. She could not doubt it now, surely? Not when he had held her in his arms and told her plainly that his feelings for her were feelings of affection.

Closing her eyes, Josephine continued with her task, feeling tears prick at her eyes. She blinked rapidly, refusing to let them fall in front of Francine. Regardless of what Lord Dunstable had said, Josephine knew that to allow herself any sort of hope was foolishness indeed. She could not let herself believe that Lord Dunstable would ever take someone like her as his bride. He had promised her that she would not be his mistress, which was what she first thought he had been suggesting, but what really could she expect from him? To have affection for her was one thing, but to be able to act upon that affection was quite another. She was nothing like Miss Georgina Wells, nothing like the kind of lady a gentleman of quality would take for a wife.

Her heart sliced into pieces as she dragged in a breath. This was ridiculous. She needed to put all such thoughts out of her head entirely. Lord Dunstable was engaged, and a gentleman did not break off an engagement without good cause. The only reason they had become close of late was due to the fever and their need to work closely with one another in order to keep the house in order and the sick cared for. Had that not occurred, then they would be worlds apart, just as they ought to be. There could be no hope for her, despite what Lord Dunstable had said.

"His fever is rising, miss."

Josephine turned at once, taking over from Gillian who immediately went to fetch a tea tray for both Josephine and Francine. Placing the cloth in the bowl, she let the mixture seep into the cloth before wringing it out and gently placing it on Lord Dunstable's forehead. Her eyes lingered on his face for a moment, feeling her heart swell with something deeper than affection. Taking a breath, she turned away for a moment, growing all the more frustrated with herself.

"Do you think he has had the fever for long?" Francine asked, softly, taking her seat beside her brother's bed. "Or did it only strike him this afternoon?"

Josephine found another cloth and placed it in the bowl, using it as a distraction so that she would not have to look at Lord Dunstable for fear that Francine would see on her face all that she was trying to hide. "He showed a little weakness and pain when we were out at the lake," she replied, thinking back to that day. "I think that was the start of it."

There was a moment of silence. "He took you to the lake?"

Josephine blushed furiously, keeping her back turned. "Indeed, but it was only to discuss the situation at the house. I had thought to return to London soon since you and your mother are both well recovered. The staff has come back and there was no appearance of the fever – until Lord Dunstable almost collapsed."

Slowly turning back around, Josephine shot a glance at Francine and saw that she was looking at her with a

CHAPTER 11

good deal of confusion on her face. "You thought to leave us, Josephine?"

"Of course," Josephine replied, beginning to gently dab Lord Dunstable's neck with the second cloth. "They will need me back at the Devil's basement in Smithfield Market. The fever still raged in London, from what I hear."

Francine reached across and grasped Josephine's hand, looking suddenly desperate. "But you will not leave us now, will you?" she asked, her voice trembling. "Not when my brother needs you."

Josephine smiled softly and set the cloth down so that she might put her free hand on top of Francine's. "I will not leave this house until your brother's fever has broken," she promised, knowing that the moment Lord Dunstable's fever left him, she would have to make plans to return to London. "I give you my word, Francine."

Francine's face crumpled. "Oh, thank you, Josephine," she whispered, letting go of Josephine's hand so that she might sit back into her seat. "I am so afraid and I do not know what to do."

Josephine frowned, a little concerned at the paleness in Francine's cheeks. "I think you can pray, my dear. You must return to your bed now, I think. You are tired and I do not want you to weaken yourself." Smiling, she moved around the bed and took Francine's arm. "Come. I will help you to your room and Gillian will bring you your tea tray in there."

"You will tell me if anything changes?" Francine asked, casting one last glance back at her brother. "And you will tell Mama what has occurred when she wakes?"

Josephine nodded, helping Francine back into her own bedchamber. "Of course I will," she said, knowing that Francine needed her reassurance. "I will not leave his side, Francine. You have my word on that."

Francine nodded and climbed back into bed, relief etched on her face. "Thank you, Josephine," she whispered, her face pale with exhaustion. "I know I can trust you."

Some hours later and Josephine felt herself grow tired also. She had spoken to Lady Dunstable, who had been shocked and horrified at the news, but who also had taken it with an abundance of steady resolve to do all she could to aid her son. Josephine had elicited a promise from the lady also, that she would not do more than she was able, given her still weakened state. However, Lady Dunstable had come to sit with her son for an hour or so, so that Josephine might eat and rest for a time. Now it was late and Josephine had sent Lady Dunstable and Francine to bed, promising each of them to rouse them should there be any news.

Not that there was any particular change with Lord Dunstable.

Josephine dipped her cloth back into the bowl of water and rested it gently on Lord Dunstable's forehead, watching the drips trail down over his temples. He muttered something incomprehensible and shifted his head back and forth on the pillow.

"Hush," Josephine soothed, running the cloth over his cheeks and down his neck, trying to bring his temperature down. "You are all right, Lord Dunstable. You are safe." She saw him twist and turn his head again, his lips moving but no sound coming out. Hating that he was in such distress and that there was very little else she could do, Josephine inclined her head and let out a long breath, feeling herself tremble just a little. She did not want him to grow weak and tired, as her parents had done, only for the fever to take the last of their strength.

In the loneliness and the growing dark of the room, Josephine felt herself fall close to despondency. She was struggling to escape from her own fears, worried that despite all of her assurances to Lady Dunstable and Miss Peters, Lord Dunstable would not survive the scarlet fever. Yes, he was strong and yes, he had as much care and attention as she and the others could give him, but deep down, Josephine was worried about how the last few weeks had affected him. He had not been at his best, having worked tirelessly looking after the house and stable, his mother, his sister, and the ill servants. Whilst he was what she would consider, a healthy and strong gentleman, he had been working himself to exhaustion of late. Would that mean that the fever could take a stronger hold?

Her eyes closed tightly as tears began to form. She had not cried in a long time, knowing that she needed to keep herself strong as she worked with those who battled this dreadful disease. To have seen so much death and so much suffering, Josephine would have thought that she would have been able to remain strong when faced with Lord Dunstable, but she found that her strength began to slowly shatter. Even though she knew she could not stay here, even though she knew that to stay here, in his house, by his side, was nothing more than a foolish dream, she was terrified that he would be taken from this life and placed in the next. What would Francine and Lady Dunstable do then?

He is engaged.

Tears crept through her closed eyelashes and brushed onto her cheeks, refusing to be held back. The truth of what Francine had told her tore at her heart again, aware that Lord Dunstable had not told her anything of the sort. Why had he said nothing to her? Why had he held her in his arms and told her of his heart's affection when he was already betrothed to another? She ought to be angry with him, ought to turn away from him entirely and let her heart settle in its loneliness once more but looking at him now, seeing him so weak and so in need of her aid, she could feel nothing but a desperate affection that longed for him to recover, even though there was no future for them both.

"Oh, Dunstable," she whispered, a small smile on her lips as she recalled how he had asked her to use his name in such an informal manner. "Why did you not tell me about her?"

There was no immediate answer, although Lord Dunstable seemed to settle a little. She found his hand amongst the bedsheets and held it, wishing that he could open his eyes and coherently explain to her why he had done such a thing. Lowering her head to her chest, Josephine gave into her sadness and her confusion, letting tears fall from her eyes as her body shook with sobs.

There was no-one to hear her, no-one to comfort her. Aside from Lord Dunstable, she was entirely alone.

"Josephine?"

Her breath caught and she lifted her head to see Lord Dunstable looking at her with half-closed eyes, his breathing quick and fast.

"Dunstable," she breathed, her fingers tightening in his as she half rose to her feet, leaning over to look at him. "You should have something to drink. Here."

Holding the small glass of water to his lips, she waited patiently for him to swallow, which he eventually did. One hand went to his throat and he groaned softly, his eyes fluttering closed.

"Dunstable?" she murmured, gently, brushing his hair from his forehead. "Can you drink any more? You must try to get your temperature down."

There came a few minutes of complete silence and Josephine, believing that Lord Dunstable had returned to his delirium, sat back in her chair whilst still keeping a hold of his hand. He had already had his medication, but he would soon need another dose, which she was all ready to supply him with. Once they passed the ninth day, *if* they managed to pass the ninth day, then Josephine would expect him to recover. For the moment, all she could do was wait.

"Josephine."

His voice was thin, barely loud enough for her to hear and yet, despite herself, Josephine leaned forward, her right hand already in his. "Yes, Lord Dunstable?" she asked, softly. "I am here, my lord."

Slowly, almost painfully, his eyes flickered open and, much to Josephine's surprise, fixed on her face.

"You are a wonderful creature," Lord Dunstable announced, evidently trying to put as much firmness into his voice as he could. "You have my heart, Josephine. I love you."

Closing her eyes, Josephine let the tears fall to her cheeks before looking at Lord Dunstable again. She did not know what to say and certainly did not know how to react, given his profession of love from his delirious state. It brought such joy to her heart and yet that joy was tinged with sadness, knowing that she could never expect him to say such a thing to her again when he was in his right mind. He was betrothed to another and, even if they did care for each other, it could never be.

Her heart was broken and, as she wiped away her tears and picked up her cloth once more, Josephine found she could not take her hand away from his. Even if it was only for a short while, she would give all the love and affection she could to this man, praying that her efforts would not come to naught and that he would be restored, in time, to his family – and his bride to be.

CHAPTER TWELVE

"I think his fever has broken."

Lady Dunstable jumped up from her chair, her hands at her mouth as Josephine came into the room. Francine's eyes filled with tears as she moved towards Josephine, putting out her hand to take hers.

"Is it true?" Francine whispered, breathlessly. "You think he will recover?"

"I am sure of it," Josephine replied, softly. "Let me change the bedsheets and ensure that he is comfortable and then you will be able to see him."

Lady Dunstable and Francine both broke down in tears at this news, hugging one another as Josephine left the room, their relief matching her own. She had been by Lord Dunstable's side for a good many days, going between fear and hope, only to see his fever disappear as his body finally broke into a sweat. Then his eyes had opened and he had looked at her, his voice rasping as he had tried to say her name. There had been no confusion there, no tossing of his head or twisting of his body as the fever ravaged him. Instead, there was understanding and clarity shining in his eyes, his hand reaching for hers.

Closing her eyes, Josephine steadied herself against the wall for a moment. She'd taken his hand for a moment and smiled at him, leaving Gillian to feed him broth whilst she went to speak to Lady Dunstable and Francine. The deep emotion she felt running through her had been enough to overwhelm her but she'd had no other choice but to keep those feelings at bay. With a great effort, she'd set her shoulders and spoken calmly to Lady Dunstable, revealing none of her own relief and heartbreak.

It was time for her to depart.

Pushing herself away from the wall, Josephine walked the length of the hallway and into Lord Dunstable's bedchamber, seeing him already sitting up as Gillian finished fluffing up his pillows. Jones was folding a stack of sheets by the end of the bed and Josephine realized that, in her absence, the butler had organized some of the staff in order to change the bedsheets already.

"Thank you, Jones," she said, softly. "Lady Dunstable and Francine will be along in a moment or two. Might you send for a tea tray for them both? I think they could both do with a little fortifying!"

He smiled at her, relief etched into his expression. "Of course, Josephine. Thank you." Putting his hand on her shoulder, he blinked back tears that came into his eyes, his smile growing steadily. "You have saved the Dunstable estate," he finished, pressing her shoulder gently. "You are a marvel, my dear."

CHAPTER 12

She smiled back at him, feeling tears prick at her own eyes such was the relief in knowing that the fever was gone from the house entirely. Here, at least, it was over.

"Josephine?"

Looking over at Lord Dunstable, she made her way to his bed and sat down carefully, taking his hand as he held it out to her.

"You must rest," she said, gently. "You ought not to be sitting up so soon."

He snorted. "I have done enough lying down," he replied, although his face twisted with pain as he put one hand to his throat. "Thank you, Josephine. Whenever I looked for you, whenever I lost my way in that dreadful fever, you were always there, waiting. I could hear your voice speaking to me, soothing me, guiding me back to where I needed to go."

Swallowing the lump in her throat, Josephine tried to smile but felt tears trickling down her cheeks.

"You were concerned for me?" he asked, his voice barely louder than a whisper, as she reached for the glass of water by his bed. Holding it to his lips, she gave him a small smile through her tears.

"A little," she replied, truthfully. "But now you are recovered, Lord Dunstable, and my happiness is complete. I – I must –"

He coughed violently, his expression wracked with pain and she helped him to sit up a little more, waiting for it to pass. Then she helped him to drink a little more, settling him back against his pillows. She could stay here for a few more days without any difficulty, of course, but she knew that the sooner she left the estate, the better.

Lady Dunstable, Francine, Gillian, and Jones could take care of him just as well as she could.

"I have not forgotten what I said to you," Lord Dunstable whispered, his eyes slowly beginning to close. "I pray you have not forgotten it either, Josephine."

Pressing her lips together for a moment, Josephine made to answer, only to see that he had fallen asleep. She wanted to tell him that she had not forgotten what he had said, that she would carry those words with her always, wanted to beg him to forgive her for leaving so quickly and without saying a proper goodbye, but he would not hear her now. He would not remember what she said to him.

Closing her eyes, Josephine wiped away her tears, feeling a ball of misery sit heavily in her chest. It was time for her to leave and yet she did not want to step away from Lord Dunstable's side. Carefully, she leaned forward and, after a moment of hesitation, pressed her lips gently to his. Lightning shot through her and she caught her breath, sitting back up to see Lord Dunstable's eyes still tightly closed. He neither moved nor spoke. What she had done would go entirely unnoticed.

"Why do I love you?" she whispered, her wretchedness becoming entirely unbearable. If only she had never allowed herself to feel such a depth of affection then this moment would not be as painful as it was!

Rising to her feet, she kept her hand on his for a moment or two longer, finding the thought of separating from him for good to be more than she could bear. Her chest rose and fell with deep, gut-wrenching sobs as she slowly let her fingers pull away from his, unable to so much as turn her head to give him one final glance before she left the room. If she did so, she might lose her resolve and stay with him, prolonging the inevitable separation that would one day come.

"My dear Josephine!"

Wiping her eyes with the back of her hand, Josephine tried to stop crying but found she could not. Francine, who appeared astonished to see Josephine in such deep distress, did nothing for a moment, then embraced Josephine in a warm hug – and Josephine felt herself break down all the more.

"You are to leave us, I think," Francine whispered, softly. "Is that the cause of your distress?"

Josephine sniffed and nodded, stepping out of Francine's embrace. "I must. The Devil's basement needs me. Your brother will respond to your care. All he needs to do is rebuild his strength." Her misery grew all the more as she dropped her gaze to the floor, feeling her heart linger behind her, safe in Lord Dunstable's arms.

"You have no family," Francine said softly, her eyes searching Josephine's. "Where will you go?"

A small shrug lifted Josephine's shoulders. "Doctor Thomas says that he will find me a position somewhere, when – and if – the fever lifts from the city. He is a good man, I think."

Francine nodded, her expression troubled. "Will you write to me when you can?" she asked, her eyes filling with tears. "You have been so very good to us, Josephine, and I cannot think of never seeing you again. We owe you a great debt."

Lifting her eyes to Francine and remembering just

how unsure the lady had been of her the very first day she arrived, Josephine let out a quiet laugh. "You are very kind, Francine, but you owe me nothing. I am just glad to have your trust and your friendship. That is all that I require. To know that someone cares for me enough to ask me to write to them has brought a great peace to my heart."

Stepping closer, Francine caught Josephine's hand. "I am not the only one who cares, Josephine."

A strangled sob escaped Josephine's throat. "Please, Francine, I –"

"Will you not stay?" Francine interrupted, softly. "Will you not stay to talk to him? I can see just how much he has come to appreciate you, Josephine."

It was a moment of indecision. Josephine felt herself sway on her feet, her desire to return to Lord Dunstable's bedchamber and continue with her nursing pulling at her. And then, unbidden, came the memory of working in the Devil's basement. Those people needed her more than Lord Dunstable. He would be quite safe here, able to make a swift recovery surrounded by those who loved him. She was not called to stay here but to go and look after those who had no-one else. People just like her.

"No," she said, giving Francine a small smile. "I must go. Doctor Thomas needs me. I will write to you though, I promise."

This did not bring a smile to Francine's face, although she did nod her understanding. A tear slipped down her cheek and she pressed Josephine's hand. "Then I will let you go. Thank you, Josephine, for all you have done. You are an angel sent from heaven, I am quite sure of it. You have given us all life back again and for that, I will forever be grateful. Goodbye, my dear friend."

Josephine swallowed her tears and tried to smile despite the pain that racked her very soul. "Goodbye, Francine. I wish you all the best of health in the years to come."

∼

The Devil's basement was just as it always had been. There was the same stench of illness, the same cloying smell of death and decay and yet, as Josephine surveyed the scene, she thought that the room was a little less crowded.

"It is good to have you back," Sam muttered, putting a hand on her shoulder. "Those ladies who came to help us, they've been working as hard as they can, but we can always do with another. I know Doctor Thomas is glad to see you."

Josephine managed a smile. "I know. I spoke to him as I came in." Doctor Thomas had been hard at work but had stopped long enough to greet her and say just how glad he was to see her returned. He had asked after the Dunstable family and it had brought her a good deal of happiness to say that they had all made a good recovery.

"There are not as many as there was once," Sam said, slowly, as though able to see into her thoughts. "But they come from all over now. It don't matter whether they be from the streets or from the townhouses, they all come here now. Or anywhere they can go, really. The fever wards are full, the doctors are all either busy or sick themselves and there ain't enough beds for everyone."

"Do you think it will pass soon?" Josephine asked, glancing at the older man. "Do you think the fever will lift from the city?"

Sam shrugged. "I can't say. I hope so but that's as much as I can do. The doctor seems to think so but how long that will take, none of us can tell."

Josephine sighed and nodded, readying herself to step into the fray once more. "Then I had best go to help Doctor Thomas," she murmured, trying to find the strength to keep going despite the pain in her heart over leaving Lord Dunstable so far behind. "Excuse me, Sam."

Wandering through the basement, her eyes taking in everything, Josephine saw that what Sam had said was quite right. There were ladies lying in their rickety beds wearing gowns that were of the highest fashion, or gentlemen whose once fine coat was now being used as a pillow for their head. They came from all over, it seemed, and still Doctor Thomas was bringing in new patients almost every hour.

"Here," Doctor Thomas muttered, gesturing for Josephine to come closer. "This is a new patient, a lady of the *ton*. I've only got her name but very little else. It seems her servants and her companion all became ill with the fever, and then she herself. It was just as well one of the footmen came to find us, otherwise we might never have found them all."

Josephine shook her head, her eyes drifting over the form of the sick lady. She had flushed cheeks, a paleness about her lips and a red spotting over her neck. "The fever claims everyone," she murmured, picking up her bowl and cloth. "Has she had any of your medicines, Doctor Thomas?"

"Yes," he replied, with a grave nod. "Some. She will need more in an hour or two. Can you use your mixture to try and bring down her fever?"

"Of course." Bending down, Josephine began to dab lightly at the lady's forehead, seeing her so young and beautiful and growing angry at this terrible disease that seemed to claim so many lives. "What did you say her name was, Doctor Thomas?"

"A Miss Georgina Wells," the doctor replied, a little distracted. "Her companion is next to her, although she appears to be doing a little better."

Josephine froze in place, her mind scrambling to recall where she heard such a name before.

And then it came to her. Miss Georgina Wells was Lord Dunstable's betrothed.

Looking down at the lady, taking in her fine clothes, her blonde curls and trim figure, Josephine could easily understand why Lord Dunstable was taken with her. She was every bit the lady and Josephine was quite sure that she had the manners, etiquette and good breeding to go with it. Shaking her head, she dabbed at the lady's forehead again, feeling her heart sink to her toes all over again.

Lord Dunstable appeared back in her thoughts yet again, her mind going over all she had seen of him, all she had said and all they had shared. Her heart turned over with guilt as she thought of how close she and Lord

Dunstable had become – not that she had known that he was engaged.

"He was never to be mine anyway," she whispered to herself, as she got to her feet to add more vinegar and feverfew to the bowl. "He was always to be yours."

There was no resentment in her voice, no anger in her heart. This was just the way of things and, despite the fact that Lord Dunstable had declared his love for her, Josephine had to believe that it was simply because of the fever. Perhaps everything he had said at the lake had simply been the start of his delirium. She had to forget him entirely, she had to let her heart let go of him. There could be no more affection for him growing within her. It had to all come to an end. She had known that and yet, even as she turned back to help Miss Wells again, she knew just how difficult that was to be.

Lifting her chin, Josephine resolved to stay by Miss Wells side as much as she could. She knew how important the lady was to Lord Dunstable and she would do all she could to help her recover. That would help her heart to forget Lord Dunstable, surely, for in helping his betrothed to recover, she would have to continually face the fact that he was never to be hers. As painful as that was to be, Josephine knew it to be for the best.

"Sam," she called, as she picked up her vinegar and feverfew. "Might you be able to find me a piece of paper? I need to write a note."

Sam lifted his brows. "A note?"

"A letter," she confirmed, nodding. "I know who this lady is. She's betrothed to Lord Dunstable."

An astonished expression caught Sam's brow. "The gentleman whose house you've just come back from?"

"The very same," she replied, quickly. "Might you help me, Sam? I need to write to him so that he knows what has become of her."

Sam nodded and shuffled off, leaving Josephine to return to Miss Wells. She bathed her forehead, cheeks, and neck, seeing the red rash spreading across the lady's décolletage.

"Where am I?"

The lady's eyes fluttered open, gazing around her in confusion. Josephine put one gentle hand to Miss Wells' forehead, feeling just how hot she was. "You're being looked after," she said, not wanting to mention the words of 'the Devil's basement'. "You have the fever. I'm here to look after you."

Miss Wells groaned, her throat obviously paining her. "I have the fever?"

"But you're going to be quite well," Josephine reassured her, putting the damp cloth on her forehead. "I'm here to look after you and Lord Dunstable will be on his way to see you very soon."

Miss Wells closed her eyes again. "Gideon," she breathed, fading back into her delirium. "Yes, send for Gideon."

"I will," Josephine replied, firmly. "You need not worry, Miss Wells. Rest now. I'll be here by your side when you waken."

The lady did not stir again but seemed to fall into a fitful sleep. A little relieved by this, Josephine left the cloth on the lady's forehead and, seeing Sam coming towards her, walked over to him to collect the paper and pencil. She would write to Lord Dunstable this very night, in the hope that soon, he would be at his betrothed's side....no matter how painful that would be for her.

CHAPTER THIRTEEN

Gideon opened his eyes slowly. Sunshine was streaming in through the window and sending a warm shaft of light onto his bed, and the sight of it made him smile. There was warmth and life and beauty and he finally felt as though he had returned to it.

He had been lost in the fever. Lost in the heat and the sweat and the confusion that came with it, his throat aching painfully as his skin burned. And yet, the only thing he could recall was Josephine. Whenever he had called for her, whenever he had tossed fitfully and cried out, she had been there to comfort him. The cool cloth had taken some of the heat from his bones and the sound of her gentle voice had soothed his fractious mind. He had a lot to thank her for.

That thought made him frown. He had not seen Josephine for the last day or so but since he had done very little other than sleep and eat, he had not had the opportunity to ask Francine or his mother where she had gone. How relieved he was to know that the rest of the house was slowly getting back to normal! The fever had gone from them all, it seemed, and whilst Gideon was sorry that he had lost a maid and a footman to the fever, he was glad that the rest of the servants appeared to be quite well. For the time being, the fear and worry over his estate had gone. Things were slowly going back to how they had once been and he could not have been more grateful to Josephine for her part in it.

A small niggle began to plague his mind. Frowning, Gideon pushed himself up to sitting, trying to let himself remember whatever it was that was attempting to come to light.

I love you.

He froze in his bed, his expression one of shock as the words he had spoken to Josephine came back to him. He had said them aloud, had said them to her and yet he could not recall what her reaction had been.

Not that what he had said was a lie, of course, for he knew in his heart that he had come to love her, but to have said it aloud was quite another thing entirely. For heaven's sake, he had only just managed to find the words to explain to her that he had begun to care for her before he had become ill, but now to discover that he had confessed his love to her whilst in the grips of the fever brought Gideon a rush of anxiety.

And what of Georgina?

A flush of heat crept into Gideon's cheeks, despite the fact that no-one else was around to witness it. That was why he had stepped back from Josephine at the lake and certainly why he ought not to have said any such words of love to her. He had to deal with the situation with Georgina first. They would bring their engagement to an end and he would find himself free to care for, love and even marry whomever he wished.

And he wished for that someone to be Josephine.

It no longer stung at his mind, the thought of marrying a lady who was neither of his class nor of noble birth. In a way, the fever had shown him that they were all the same, regardless of accident of birth. Kindness, compassion, and consideration were not traits that were in the nobility alone. In fact, Josephine had shown more of these things than his own betrothed lady, who had kept entirely silent by the looks of things – and certainly was not by his side now, watching over him! Gideon found he did not care what would be said about him should he be permitted to marry Josephine. The thought of having a heart so fulfilled, a life so full of love and affection, was enough to make him want to dance about the room with joy. Class and titles be damned! Love was all he required.

"Gideon?"

He turned his head to see Francine stick her head through the ajar doorway and smiled, beckoning her in.

"Good morning, my dear sister," he said, welcoming her. "Come in. I am quite at my leisure, as you can see."

Francine had been by his side these last two days, feeding him broth when he had been too weak to do so, but Gideon knew that he would not require such nursing today. His strength was already returning in swift bounds.

"Oh, Dunstable, I have been ever so worried about you," Francine said, hurrying in and referring to him now in the way she normally did, which told Gideon that he must be looking a good deal better. "You look brighter this morning, though it can scarcely be called morning since it is very near to noon."

Smiling, he pushed himself up against the pillows, wondering if he would be able to get out of his bed this morning. "You cannot begrudge me rest, surely?"

Laughing, she shook her head. "No, indeed. You will need as much of it as you can these next few days. I know it."

Tipping his head just a little, Gideon regarded his sister. "Where is Josephine?"

The smile faded from Francine's face almost immediately. "Josephine? Why, she has gone."

A heavy weight dropped into Gideon's stomach. "Gone?" he repeated, his voice growing a little thin. "What do you mean, she is gone?"

Francine lifted one shoulder, although the look in her eyes told Gideon that she knew more than she was saying. "She waited until the fever had broken and you were making a recovery, before returning to London to the Devil's basement in Smithfield Market. The people there need her too, Dunstable."

Gideon frowned. "Yes, I know that, Francine, but I would have thought that...." He trailed off, unable to voice the rest of his words. He wanted to tell Francine that he had expected Josephine to linger here, at the house, until he was well recovered so that they might, at the very least, talk about what had transpired between them, but that was a private matter and so he could not say a word. At the same time, he did not want to appear begrudging that Josephine had returned to London, recalling the horror and the stench of the Devil's basement. Francine was right to say that those people needed Josephine's aid also.

"You wanted her to stay."

The statement was casually made but the small smile on his sister's lips spoke of understanding of all that he was feeling. He ducked his head for a moment, a little unsure as to what to say or what to do, only to feel his sister touch his hand.

"You care for Josephine, do you not?"

Sighing heavily, Gideon looked up at her and gave her a wry smile. "You will think me foolish."

"No!" Francine exclaimed at once, looking rather hurt that he would think so. "No, indeed, Dunstable, I do not. I think that she is a marvelous creature and it comes as little surprise to me that you have found your heart so caught up with her – but what about Georgina? She is your betrothed, is she not?"

Gideon closed his eyes for a moment, his breath dragging out of him. "Yes, indeed, she is. I do not know what to say to you in that regard, my dear sister, for I confess that I am in great confusion about what to do or say to my betrothed. I do not think that she cares for me one jot and I confess that I do not care for her either. That cannot be a solid foundation on which to build a marriage. I have resolved in my heart that, therefore, our engagement must come to an end. Although," he continued, shoving one hand through his hair, "how I am to tell her such a thing I cannot say, for she does not seem to want to respond to my letters. I do not even know where she resides at this present moment either!"

Francine's expression became sympathetic. "I quite understand, Dunstable. I wrote to her when you first became ill and, not knowing where she was, thought to send a copy to her father's estate with the original going to London."

Gideon frowned. "And you have heard nothing from her?"

Shaking her head, Francine eyed Gideon carefully. "And you are quite convinced that you care for Josephine?"

Looking steadily at his sister, Gideon felt his heart ring with certainly. "I love her," he said, slowly. "And I intend to marry her, Francine, if she will have me."

His sister said nothing for a moment but, taking in a breath, nodded and smiled. "Then I think you must return to London the moment you are well enough to do so," she said, firmly. "For you will need to find her there and confess it all to her."

"Once I have spoken to Georgina, I shall do so at once," Gideon replied, firmly. "Thank you, Francine."

At that very moment, the door opened and the butler hurried in, bearing a letter for Gideon. It was a rather dirty looking letter from first glance and Gideon hesitated for a moment, picking it up carefully and turning it over. There was no seal to break and so, carefully, unfolding it, he let his eyes run over the few short sentences.

His breath caught.

"What is it?" Francine asked, a little upset at seeing

her brother's face now so pale. "Is something wrong? Is it Josephine?"

"No," Gideon replied, hoarsely. "It is not Josephine. It is Georgina."

Francine stared at him. "Georgina?"

Nodding, Gideon handed his sister the letter. "It is from Josephine. She writes that she is tending to Georgina, Georgina's companion and some of the staff from the townhouse. It appears that they have all caught the fever."

One hand flew to Francine's mouth. "Goodness."

Gideon closed his eyes. He knew what his duty was and, despite the fact that he was to bring their engagement to an end, he knew he had to go to London to be by Georgina's side.

"I must write to her father and then prepare to go to London," he said, throwing back the bedcovers and swinging his legs to the ground. Attempting to stand, he felt a wave of weakness rush through him which forced him to sit back down on the edge of the bed.

Francine shook her head. "You cannot make the trip immediately, Gideon, not in your weakened state. Write to her father, yes, but prepare to leave the estate by the week's end."

"No," Gideon replied firmly, frustrated that his limbs would not do what he wished them. "I must go now."

"But you cannot," Francine replied, gently. "Gideon, you would collapse on the way to the carriage. Please, think carefully. Make preparations for the end of the week, when you will have enough strength to travel. I will come with you, of course, as will mama."

Gideon shook his head. "No, you will both remain here. London is rife with the disease and I will not endanger you again." He closed his eyes for a moment, feeling frustrated and angry that he could not go to London just as soon as he wished. "But you are right to urge me to wait. I will do so." His mind filled with thoughts of Josephine and Georgina, feeling sympathy and sadness for his betrothed. She would be enduring all that he had experienced, without any of the comforts of being at home. How she had ended up in the Devil's basement, he could not imagine, growing all the more concerned that Viscount Armitage, Georgina's father, had as yet not been heard from.

"Georgina will receive the best of care, Dunstable," Francine said, softly, one hand on his arm. "If it is Josephine caring for her then you know full well she will be taken care of. It says here in the letter that Josephine is staying by her side, day and night, with the awareness of just how important a person she is to you."

A small groan escaped Gideon's lips. He had not thought that Josephine would discover the truth about Georgina, never once letting himself consider the idea of talking to her about the matter, but now that he saw they were both together regardless, he wished he had done so.

"Did Josephine know about Georgina before she left this house?" he asked, his voice fragmented as he looked at his sister. "I had not told her and –"

"*I* told her," Francine replied, softly. "I did not mean to cause you any trouble, Dunstable."

"And is that why she left?" Gideon persisted, fixing

his sister with a stern gaze. "Is that why she turned away from me and my house?"

Francine looked back at him steadily. "I think Josephine cares for you very much, Dunstable," she replied, softly. "But she believes that her place can never be by your side."

"And I cannot blame her for that," Gideon sighed, flopping back against his pillows. "This is becoming a somewhat twisted mess, is it not?"

Francine smiled sympathetically. "Go to London, Dunstable. See how Georgina fares. The most important thing at this present moment is that she recovers. After that, you will have to see what comes of it all."

CHAPTER FOURTEEN

*J*osephine looked up to see two figures coming into the basement, her breath catching in her chest as she realized it was none other than Lord Dunstable, accompanied by Sam. Sam was indicating the bed near to where Josephine stood and she moved away at once, unable to be in Lord Dunstable's presence. She could not bear to have him look at her, could not bear to have him see her standing there, in her dirty gown and matted hair whilst he looked after his dear bride to be.

Her heart ached as she stumbled away into the shadowy darkness, neither wanting to be seen or heard. Doctor Thomas was with Georgina at the moment which meant she had no reason to linger. There were plenty of others who needed her.

And yet, as she stepped away, her heart filled with relief and gladness that she had seen Lord Dunstable so restored to health and strength. It was a very strange sensation, to be so filled with delight and yet feel so much pain in equal measure. Closing her eyes for a moment, she put one hand on the grimy wall, steadying herself. She knew that he would come, hadn't she? The moment she'd sent him a note to say that Miss Wells was here, she'd known that he would come to her. To see him now, so worried and concerned over his betrothed, brought a fresh stab of pain to her heart. She had been so foolish to think that what he had confessed to her was the truth of his heart. It had been words from the depths of his delirium and nothing more.

"How is she faring, doctor?"

Lord Dunstable's voice filled the basement and Josephine had to drag in yet another breath, feeling as though she wanted to run far from this place. She could not bear to hear him speak, could not bear to lay her eyes on him and yet she knew there was no escape.

"She is doing a good deal better, my lord," Doctor Thomas replied, with a hint of relief in his voice. "The fever broke only this morning. I think that soon, she will be able to return home to rest and recover there."

Josephine let out her breath slowly, going in search of her cloths so that she might start tending to others. Let Lord Dunstable and the doctor speak. That part of her life was over now and the sooner she forgot about Lord Dunstable, all the better.

"You have Josephine to thank for her care, however," she heard the doctor say, freezing in place as he spoke. "That girl has barely left Miss Wells side since the moment she came in. She stated that she knew how much the lady meant to you, my lord."

There was silence from Lord Dunstable and Josephine remained exactly where she was, bowl in hand, unable to do so much as turn her head to see if he was searching for her in the gloom of the basement.

"Josephine is a marvel," Lord Dunstable said, eventually, his voice a little louder than before as though he wanted to ensure she heard every word he said. "I cannot thank her enough for what she has done – both in my own house and now here. She is an angel."

Doctor Thomas let out a long breath. "I would agree," he replied, as Josephine managed to throw him a quick glance over her shoulder, her breath coming out raggedly as the threat of tears began to grow all the more. "I do not know what I would have done without her."

Josephine could not listen to anymore. The urge to run to Lord Dunstable and throw her arms around him, to tell him that she was so very glad to see him happy and safe once more grew steadily, and yet the knowledge that he was to marry Georgina Wells threw all that into disarray. He was not hers to embrace. He was not hers to love. He belonged to another and she could never take her place.

Brushing tears from her eyes, Josephine set down the bowl with a clang and, unable to look at anyone, quickly made her way from the basement. Climbing the stairs, she moved into the church itself, not daring to go outside just in case Lord Dunstable should follow her out.

The church was quiet and she crept into a pew,

feeling the hard wood against her back as she sat down. There seemed to be no-one else present. She didn't know where the vicar was or what had become of him. Had he caught the fever too? Was he lying sick somewhere?

The enormity of the present situation swam over her, forcing her to bow her head. The fever had swept through the city and taken so many lives and, whilst she had done as much as she could, there was always more for her to do. The life she had once had with Lord Dunstable, as tiring as it was, had been a taste of an altogether different existence and, for a time, she had lost herself in that. She had let her heart feel things she ought never to have allowed herself to feel, had let her mind dream of what she might have with Lord Dunstable. It was all her own fault. She had not remained detached and unaffected as she should have done.

Even now, memories assailed her. Memories of talking and laughing with Lord Dunstable. Memories of sitting with him quietly, praying silently that the fevers of his mother and sister would break. Memories of how they had shared together, learning from one another and finding an intimacy she had never experienced before. All gone, now, just as it should. Her life in the Dunstable estate had never been meant to continue. She had, for a time, forgotten that.

"Josephine."

Looking up, Josephine felt her breath hitch as Lord Dunstable stood at the end of the pew, looking at her with such a joyful expression on his face that she felt her heart break all over again. He was glad that Miss Wells was recovering, which, of course, she was too – but there was something more there. It was a love in his eyes, she thought to herself, unable to look at him any longer. Turning her head away, she forced herself not to cry, forced herself to remain strong as he came to sit by her, his closeness only adding to her agony.

He loved Miss Wells. It was obvious to her now. Foolish, foolish woman that she was! She had taken what he had said in the depths of his delirium and had believed it to be true, even if only for a moment. There had been a hope flickering in her heart ever since then, refusing to be quenched no matter how much she had told herself that she was being ridiculous.

Now, however, it had died completely. Seeing the love in Lord Dunstable's eyes had only confirmed what she'd never really wanted to believe. He loved Miss Wells, the woman of quality he was to marry. Miss Wells, who was proper in every way, she had no doubt. Not compared to her, the urchin from the streets who had nothing and nobody to call her own.

She sniffed and heard Lord Dunstable sigh heavily.

"My goodness, Josephine, we are in a muddle," he said, slowly. "But I came here to thank you for what you have done for Georgina. And for me."

Nodding, she kept her gaze trained on her feet, unable to look at him for fear she would break down completely. "You are quite welcome, Lord Dunstable. I knew how much she meant to you."

There was a short pause. One where Lord Dunstable did not either confirm nor deny what Josephine had said.

"Francine told you about her?" he asked, a little stiffly.

"She did," Josephine confirmed, hating that her voice was shaking just a little.

He sighed. "I should have done so myself. I –"

"You are not obliged to tell me anything, Lord Dunstable," Josephine interrupted, not wanting to be reminded of how close they had become. "I was merely in your house for a time to help your mother and sister with the fever. I am glad I was able to do so."

Much to her horror, Lord Dunstable reached across and took her hand. Her heart burst to life as their fingers met, his touch already so familiar and yet so unwelcome. She wanted to lean into him, wanted to cry out that she had missed him desperately, that she had clung onto his words for so long – but instead, she sat stiffly, forcing herself not to outwardly react.

"I should have spoken to you about Georgina," Lord Dunstable said, softly, his fingers tightening on hers. "It was wrong of me to confess my feelings when I am engaged to another. I am sorry, Josephine."

She did not know what to make of this, confusion spiraling through her mind. His feelings? Did that mean that he had, at one time at least, felt something for her?

"Things are very different now," he continued, a little sadness tinging his words. "I must care for Georgina. Her father cannot be found and I fear that he too has the fever – although where he might be I cannot tell."

"I see," Josephine replied, not knowing what else to say on the matter.

"I think that I should remove Georgina to her townhouse as soon as she is able," Lord Dunstable continued, although why he was telling Josephine such things as this, she could not quite understand. "Her companion is a little recovered also, although it will take some time for her to regain her strength. There is a good deal I must do. I must find Georgina's father, Viscount Armitage, for one. In addition, I must continue to ensure that Georgina receives the highest care."

Josephine nodded blindly, her eyes unseeing as she heard him speak. She would not see him again after this. Their time together was over for good and, in a way, Josephine was glad.

"Will you come with me, Josephine?"

His question shot a lightning bolt through her and she sat bolt upright, turning tear-filled eyes onto him.

"I know it is a lot to ask of you, but Georgina needs the highest level of care. There is no-one better than you."

She closed her eyes tightly, feeling one single tear fall onto her cheek. "No, my lord," she replied, knowing that as much as she wanted to help Georgina, she could not bring herself to see Lord Dunstable with his bride to be. "I cannot. There are people here who need me."

His disappointment was immediately evident. "I quite understand," he replied, his shoulders slumping. "I should not be selfish, I know, but –"

"She is important to you, I quite understand," Josephine interrupted, wishing desperately that their conversation would be at an end so that Lord Dunstable would leave her to her misery. "You need not explain."

There was a short, strained silence.

CHAPTER 14

"Our engagement was arranged."

She looked at him then, her tears drying on her cheek.

"I had very little choice in the matter and, until some weeks ago, I did not think that it mattered all that much. However, now, I find myself struggling. Struggling to know what is best to do, what is *right* for me to do." His eyes met hers, his fingers beginning to thread through her own. "Josephine, can you forgive me?"

She did not know what precisely it was that he was asking her to forgive him for and so stared at him blankly.

"I should have been open with you from the start," he confessed, seeing her expression. "I should have spoken to you about Georgina but my heart and my mind have been warring for some time and it all became much too confusing. I am sorry, Josephine."

Somehow, she managed to nod and give him a small smile, which, despite the tearing of her heart, he seemed to accept.

"What will you do now?" he asked, rising to his feet. "When the Devil's basement no longer needs you?"

She did not move but stayed exactly where she was, longing to be alone. "The doctor has said he will help me. I trust him to do that."

"The doctor is a good man," Lord Dunstable said, softly. "I am glad he will care for you, Josephine. Again, thank you for all you have done. I do not think I can ever find the words to express just how grateful I am. You are an angel sent to help me and my family and what you have done can never be praised highly enough."

Her eyes fastened on him, wanting to keep a hold of

him for as long as she could and yet knowing that their parting was imminent. "I pray you will all remain in excellent health for the rest of your days," she said, not quite sure what else to say. "Thank you, Lord Dunstable."

With a swift suddenness, he came back towards her, leaning over and kissing her cheek. His lips lingered there for a moment too long and Josephine's breath caught. His nearness, his closeness, burned into her mind and her soul, her eyes closing tightly against the flood of tears.

And then, he was gone.

Josephine let out a ragged breath, fighting back the sobs that threatened to overwhelm her. Lord Dunstable would take Miss Wells back to her townhouse and then, in time, back to his estate as his wife. The foolish dream she had once allowed herself to create now shattered all around her, the pieces piercing her skin as they fell.

She had to let him go. She had to forget him, to push him from her heart and let go of all that she felt. There was nothing for her and Lord Dunstable to share, not any longer.

Her life would remain here, on the streets of London, whilst Lord Dunstable remained in his wonderful estate, in a life far removed from her own. They were worlds apart once again, completely separated and this time, for good.

It was an hour or so before Josephine felt able to leave the church and descend back down into the Devil's basement. It was certainly growing quieter, with fewer and fewer patients being brought in to be cared for. She paused in the doorway for a moment, looking over the place that had become so familiar to her and was yet so terrible.

The other ladies who had come to help were soon not to be needed. Two had already left, their employment as maids having been returned to them. The other two would go soon too, Josephine thought to herself, knowing that they had a place to go. She, however, had nowhere to call her own. There was no home to return to, no family to welcome her in. All she had was Doctor Thomas' kindness and assurance that he would not see her out on the streets again.

Of course, the other thing she had was Lord Dunstable's coins, given to her so long ago. They were safe and secure, but she felt as though she did not want to use them. They would only continue to remind her of him, everything she bought, everything she used, would bring him back to her mind.

That was not what she wanted.

"Josephine?"

She looked up to see Sam coming near her, a worried expression on his face.

"Are you all right?"

"I'm fine, Sam," she replied, with a quick smile, hoping that the dim light hid her red-rimmed eyes. "How is the doctor doing?"

Sam tipped his head. "Better today, I should think. There aren't so many new patients and he's been able to send a few more back home to recover. That Miss Wells is to be going tomorrow."

Josephine let her eyes rest on where Miss Wells, now half sitting up against the somewhat dirty pillows, was looking up at Doctor Thomas with an expression of sheer gratitude on her face.

"Doctor Thomas has done wonders for her," she said quietly, feeling no anger or upset about the lady's presence here. "I am glad she has recovered."

"So, it seems, is Doctor Thomas," Sam murmured, one eyebrow lifted. "He's been spending a bit more time with her that his other patients, that's for certain."

Surprised, Josephine turned to Sam expecting to see him laughing but he was doing no such thing. Instead, he was watching the scene in front of them with an almost calculated expression, as though able to surmise what the doctor intended for Miss Wells.

"I hardly think that is fair to the doctor," Josephine said, quietly. "He is a good man and not likely to show favor to one lady simply because she is gentry."

Sam chuckled, putting his hand on her shoulder. "No, of course not. That's not what I meant."

"Then what did you mean?" Josephine asked, feeling confused. "I don't understand."

Sam chuckled again and shook his head. "It doesn't matter. Look sharp now, the doctor's coming over."

Josephine rolled her eyes at Sam, her spirits lifting from their gloom at his good humor. "Doctor Thomas," she began, turning her gaze back to the doctor. "What is it that you need me to do?"

Doctor Thomas smiled, his expression looking a good deal brighter than she had ever seen before. "It looks as though the epidemic is finally lifting," he said, his eyes filled with relief. "Miss Wells is to be taken back to her townhouse tomorrow morning and I will visit there each afternoon and evening, to ensure that her recovery continues without any problems."

A little surprised, Josephine felt rather than saw Sam's sharp glance, but deliberately kept her expression blank. "I see," she replied, calmly. "Her father's house is nearby, isn't it?"

The doctor nodded. "It is. With fewer patients, I feel as though I can leave here now and again and let you take over. That is not going to overwhelm you, is it?"

Josephine shook her head. "No, of course not. I understand completely."

The doctor let out a long sigh. "It will be good for me to get out of this place for a time," he said, running one hand through his hair as he turned to look at the remaining patients. "I have had quite enough of living in a basement filled with disease and death."

His voice took on a haunted tone and, for the first time, Josephine realized just how much of a strain this had been to Doctor Thomas. She felt her heart go out to him, her admiration growing steadily.

"You have been a blessing to so many people, Doctor Thomas," she said, softly. "I know that there are many who owe their lives to you."

Doctor Thomas gave a half shrug, his expression wry. "I will choose not to reflect on how many we lost," he replied, his voice a little thin. "But yet, Josephine, I will be glad to leave this place behind. I have not forgotten you, either. You will have a room of your own that is connected to my practice, so long as you are still willing to aid me in my work?"

Relief enveloped Josephine and she nodded fervently, filled with the knowledge that she would, at least, have a home and a purpose in life. She would not end up on the streets again. Doctor Thomas had been faithful to his word.

"I would be glad to, Doctor," she replied, as Sam grinned at her. "Thank you."

Doctor Thomas nodded, before glancing over his shoulder to where Miss Wells lay, her face puckered in a frown.

"She needs something to drink and a little more broth," he muttered, half to himself. "I should help her. Excuse me."

Josephine nodded and watched him go, feeling a good deal happier than she had been.

"I will miss you," Sam murmured, his voice now a little hoarse as he evidently battled with his emotions. "We've become like family, these last few weeks."

Josephine turned to him, her heart stopping for a moment. "Where will you go, Sam?"

He shrugged. "The doctor don't need me, Josephine. I'll find my own way somehow."

"I'm sure Doctor Thomas would be more than happy to help you," Josephine insisted. "I know he –"

Sam help up one hand. "He's offered but I refused," he interrupted, gently. "The doctor is a kind man and gave me some coins to help me on my way, when I wouldn't accept his offer. I'll find my own way in the world, just like I always have done."

CHAPTER 14

Josephine shook her head. "Sam, no. You cannot just go back to the London streets, not after all you have done." A sudden thought caught her mind. "Why not ask Lord Dunstable for employment?"

Sam laughed harshly. "And what would I do? I can't be a footman!"

"The gardener, then. Or a stable hand!" Josephine exclaimed, refusing to let the idea drop. "Please, Sam. Let me help you in the same way that you've helped so many."

There was a long silence before Sam, finally, nodded.

"Thank you," Josephine breathed, one hand on his arm. "I know he'd be glad to help you, Sam. He's a good, kind man and I know he'll have something for you to do."

"If you say so," Sam replied, a touch doubtfully.

"I'll write the letter today and have Doctor Thomas hand it to him when Miss Wells is taken home tomorrow," Josephine replied, firmly. "Don't you worry, Sam. You'll have a place of your own too, soon enough."

Sam let out a slow breath and Josephine was surprised to see tears sparkling in his eyes. She'd known that Sam had always had a bit of a difficult life, what with his limp, but had never imagined that the thought of returning to it would be so difficult.

"I'll miss you all the more," Sam muttered, dashing one hand over his eyes. "You're a blessing to everyone who surrounds you, Josephine. Don't you go forgetting that."

She smiled and put her hand on his. "Thank you, Sam," she replied, quietly, her heart no longer as pained and as sore as it had once been. Perhaps she did have a family, in a way. She did have friends and now, she had a place to stay and a purpose for her life. In time, what she felt for Lord Dunstable would fade and she would find her heart free once more. For the moment, she would simply endure.

CHAPTER FIFTEEN

"How is she, Doctor Thomas?"
Doctor Thomas came down the last few steps and inclined his head as he came near to Gideon. "She is improving slowly, my lord. I have given her some medicine and the maid is now feeding her broth. Miss Wells will require a good rest thereafter, so I would not disturb her for some hours." Setting down his bag, he let out a long breath. "I fear that she may be weakened for a prolonged length of time, however. She may require a good deal of care and may never have a strong constitution again."

Gideon swallowed, his once happy future slowly evaporating. He had once had the intention of coming to London to speak to Georgina in order to bring their engagement to an end so that he might declare himself to Josephine, but now that moment had passed. He could not turn his back on Georgina now, not when it was obvious she needed someone desperately. She needed him to take care of her, to help restore her to her full strength – just as Josephine had done for his mother, his sister and for him.

"She *will* recover, my lord," Doctor Thomas said, gently, putting one hand on Gideon's arm, thinking him to be distraught over Georgina's condition. "It will just take time."

Gideon smiled and nodded, shaking off his dark thoughts. This was not the time to be selfish and to consider all he had lost and all that could have been. This was the time to consider Georgina and what it was *she* required of him. He had made a promise and now it was time for him to fulfill it.

He would marry her, just as he had agreed. The love he felt for Josephine would have to linger on in his heart and mind but it would never find fulfillment. It was nothing more than a dark, painful memory that caught at his mind and tore at it, hard. He would never be able to make her his wife. That was a dream he would have to forget. Georgina was his future and he was determined now to be entirely devoted to that.

"I have sent some of my men out to see if they can find her father," he explained, as the doctor picked up his bag. "I fear he too has fallen ill with the fever, for he is not in his estate nor is he in London."

The doctor nodded slowly, his expression grave. "Miss Wells has been asking for him but I thought it best to leave such questions to you," he replied, quietly. "I will come back this evening to see how she fares, if that pleases you."

"Of course," Gideon exclaimed at once. "Georgina must have the best of care, doctor."

The doctor smiled. "And so she shall. Oh, I almost forgot." He pulled a piece of paper from his pocket and handed it to Gideon. "Josephine has written to you and asked me to deliver it. She hopes you will be able to give her an answer by this evening."

Gideon's heart picked up speed. "An answer?" he repeated, looking at the letter in confusion. "About what?"

Chuckling, the doctor lifted one shoulder. "She would not say but I hardly think it will be anything too terrible, my lord," he replied, as Gideon tried to wipe the astonished expression from his face. "Josephine is a remarkable young woman and I am quite sure that whatever it is contained in that letter will be for either your good or someone else's."

"Where is she to go, once this epidemic lifts?" Gideon asked, unable to prevent himself from ensuring that Josephine would be quite safe. "Does she have somewhere to go?"

A smile caught Doctor Thomas' lips. "She is to help me, Lord Dunstable. I have a small practice with a room adjoining it that currently lies empty. She can live there and assist me with the daily workings of the practice."

Gideon nodded, feeling almost hollow inside as he realized just how far apart their worlds would be, once again. "I am glad to hear it."

"I would not let her go back onto the streets, not after the work she has done," Doctor Thomas finished, putting on his hat. "It is good of you to think of her, my lord."

"How could I not, after all she did for my family?" Gideon asked, a little hoarsely. "Thank you for this letter, doctor. Please assure Josephine that I will have my answer ready and waiting for you this evening."

The doctor smiled, nodded and excused himself, leaving Gideon standing alone in the hallway with the letter in his hand. The letter that Josephine had written.

Looking down at it, Gideon felt his heart fill with thoughts of her all over again. He was so desperately torn and yet he knew that he really did not have any particular choice in what he did as regarded his engagement. It would have been quite different had Georgina not become ill but as things now stood, he had no opportunity to step away from it as he had planned.

Feeling the need to be somewhere private, Gideon walked into the empty drawing-room, sat down by the fire and opened the letter. Reading it quickly, he felt his shoulders slump, his spirits sinking low. There was no profession of love, no words of sweetness or the like – not that he should have expected there to be, of course, given that he had already made his position quite clear to her. Instead, she was simply asking that he extend a kindness towards the older man who had been working at the Devil's basement alongside herself and Doctor Thomas. Sam, his name was, and whilst Josephine made it clear that he would never be a footman or valet, she thought he would do well as a stable hand or gardener.

It was not in Gideon's heart to refuse. He knew who Sam was, recalling how the older man had limped slightly as he'd made his way from bed to bed. He had always presumed that Sam had somewhere to go once the epidemic was over, but perhaps he had been wrong.

Sighing heavily, he folded up the letter and put it back in his pocket. He would, of course, write to Josephine and ensure that Sam was taken back to his estate, once the disease had enjoyed its fill of London. To give the older man a livelihood and security was the least Gideon could do, after all Sam had done to help others.

Rubbing his hand over his eyes, Gideon tried to let all he thought and felt for Josephine simply fade away. He longed to feel something for Georgina, even in her weakened state, but his heart simply refused to warm to her. She was not Josephine. That was the crux of it. As far as Gideon was concerned, there was no other. And yet, to do what was right meant having both his and Josephine's heart broken.

He had no doubt that Josephine cared for him also, even though she had not said as much. The memories of the time they'd spent together lingered on in his mind and Gideon smiled to himself as he thought of them. How she had laughed when he'd tried to help her with the cooking, mocking him gently and bringing a flush of heat to his face. He had not known what to do or how to help but had done his best to do so and she had appreciated him for that. When they had walked down by the lake, he had felt his thoughts so much in turmoil that he had struggled to get those words of affection from his lips and yet she had not turned away from him. She had stayed in his arms, looking at him as though he were both the most wonderful and the most terrifying man in the world.

Of course, then the fever had taken him and he had lost himself within it, only to declare his love for her in a single moment of clarity before delving back into his delirium. At least she knew that he cared for her, he thought, his brows furrowing together as he remembered being lost in the heat and the pain of the fever.

And then, something else came into his mind.

A kiss.

His eyes closed tightly as he struggled to bring that memory back completely. A kiss? He had not kissed Josephine, had he? Surely he had not had the strength to raise himself from his bed and press his lips to hers! Which meant that it must have been she who had kissed him.

Trying to still himself completely, Gideon let his mind fill with nothing but thoughts of Josephine. Slowly, it began to come clear in his mind. He had felt the sensation of her lips on his and had not been able to move, had not been able to reciprocate despite the desperate longing of his heart.

"Why do I love you?"

His lips spoke the words aloud, the cloud of darkness clearing for a moment as he remembered what she had whispered just after she had kissed him. Her wretched words brought him a sharp pain, realizing just how tormented she had been in the knowledge that she loved him but yet would never be able to find the fulfillment of that love. His breathing was ragged as he opened his eyes, startled to find dampness on his cheeks. This memory, whilst wonderful, had made it all the more painful to him. Their love was to be unrequited, it seemed. He had gone from a man who did not think that love was of any importance to a marriage, to being a man so deeply in love that he could hardly bear the thought of being without it. He sat back and let the tears come. They flowed down his cheeks, unabated, bringing with them the fresh sting of a broken heart.

"I am to retire, I think."

Gideon saw the butler bow and noted how pale the gentleman was. "I think you should ensure that both you and the rest of your staff rest well this evening," Gideon continued, with a little more firmness than perhaps the butler intended, for he started visibly and looked aghast at Gideon.

"If I have been failing in my duties, my lord, then I can only apologize," the man stammered, still horrified by what Gideon had suggested. "I –"

"No, no, you quite misunderstand me," Gideon replied, with a broad smile. "I do not mean that you and the staff are doing poorly, but rather that I know full well what it is like to recover from scarlet fever." He saw the butler visibly relax and got to his feet, wanting to calm the gentleman further. "You are short of staff, I know, but I only intend to reside here with Miss Georgina and her companion for a short time. Then, when her companion is well enough to take care of Miss Georgina, I shall return to my estate to make the necessary preparations for her there, once we are wed. You must not overburden yourself or the rest of the staff during this time. I am quite content, truly."

The butler inclined his head, his features a good deal more relaxed. "I quite understand, my lord," he replied, quietly. "I thank you for your consideration. I will make sure the staff take a rest tomorrow morning, as you have suggested."

"And I will not require anything until noon, I should think," Gideon replied, glancing at the clock and realizing just how late it was. "And even then, it will just be coffee and something simple to eat."

The butler nodded. "Of course, my lord. Is there anything else?"

"No. I thank you." Dismissing the butler, Gideon looked about the drawing room for his book and, picking it up, made his way to the door. Walking quickly up the staircase to where his bedchamber was – as far away from Miss Georgina's bedchamber as possible, Gideon reflected on the fact that were things as they normally were in London, this would all be seen as quite improper. Georgina's reputation would be ruined and they would have been wed almost immediately. However, as things stood, this was perfectly acceptable, especially since Georgina's father could not be found.

Making sure to walk quietly along the hallway so as not to disturb Georgina, whom he expected to be sleeping, Gideon was suddenly caught by the sound of voices coming from her bedchamber. Thinking that it was a chattering maid, he made to turn around and give the young girl a piece of his mind, instructing her that the lady of the house needed to rest, only to come to a dead stop as he realized there was a low voice coming from the room. This was no maid, and it certainly was not

Georgina's companion who, from the sound of the snores coming from the next bedchamber, was not sitting with Georgina, deep in conversation.

"Really, Doctor Thomas, you are jesting!"

Gideon blinked rapidly, a little surprised to hear Georgina's voice so filled with life when she had barely said a word to him that afternoon when he had visited her. Indeed, she had been sitting up against the pillows but had not looked as though she wished to talk with him. He had tried for some minutes to ask her how she was and what he might do for her, but she had simply stated that she was quite all right but a little tired and needed to rest. Of course, understanding the weakness that came after the fever, he had left her be but now to hear her talking and laughing with Doctor Thomas, it made Gideon wonder whether or not she had been entirely truthful with him.

"Are you to stay in London, Miss Wells?"

Gideon closed his eyes, trying to force himself to step away, to leave the conversation to be between Doctor Thomas and Georgina alone, and yet he could not.

"Please, Doctor Thomas, do call me Georgina," he heard Georgina say. "You have done so much for me already and I do find the propriety of it all a little ridiculous when I am here, practically swaddled in sheets!"

Doctor Thomas chuckled. "Very well then. Georgina, it is." There was a short pause and even Gideon, from where he stood, felt it laden with an almost anticipatory tension.

"Then tell me, Georgina," Doctor Thomas continued, his voice a little lower than before. "Are you to remain in London for some time, or are you to return to Lord Dunstable's estate very soon?"

Georgina sighed heavily. "I will remain here until I have recovered enough strength to leave, Doctor Thomas."

"I see." Again, another pause and it was all Gideon could do not to look into the room to see what they were about.

"Then I will come and see you again tomorrow afternoon," Doctor Thomas continued, his manner a little more brisk. "I will need to try and ensure that you recover as quickly as possible, Miss Wells. I cannot imagine that you are eager to delay your wedding."

Georgina said nothing and, after a moment, Gideon heard the chair behind pushed just a little as the doctor rose to his feet.

"I should return to the church now," Doctor Thomas said, quietly. "I have taken up too much of your time and you need to rest, Miss Wells. I –"

"No, Doctor Thomas, please."

Startled, Gideon lifted his brows in surprise. Was Georgina asking the doctor to stay longer?

"Might you sit with me for a short while? I am not yet tired and I feel as though I am in desperate need of company."

Doctor Thomas cleared his throat. "Perhaps I might go in search of Lord Dunstable, Miss Wells."

"Georgina," she insisted, a little more firmly. "And no, you need not bother him. I am quite sure my fiancé has retired already, Doctor Thomas. Please, will you not sit with me?"

Her voice had become almost wheedling and Gideon felt his teeth set on edge. He disliked that about Georgina intently, hating that she could so often use such a thing to try and force him to do as she asked.

Doctor Thomas, however, did not appear to be displeased by it. "Then, I shall stay if you ask it of me," he said, slowly, the sound of the chair scraping along the floor catching Gideon's ears. "But only for a short time. There are others that I need to see, Georgina."

"Thank you," she said, a good deal more gently. "I must say that I have been enjoying your company of late, Doctor Thomas. Thank you for being so willing to sit with me."

"You are quite welcome," Doctor Thomas replied, his voice now a little softer than before. "Now, what shall we talk about?"

Gideon did not want to linger. Instead, he turned on his heel and carefully and quietly made his way back towards his own bedchamber instead of lingering at Georgina's. He had his own opinion about his betrothed so openly seeking the company and conversation of a doctor so late into the night, but then again, he could not exactly criticize her for doing so when he had done almost the very same with Josephine.

Wandering back to his bedchamber, Gideon felt his mind begin to flood with questions, finding himself rather unsettled by what he had just overheard. Of course, there came with that a good dose of guilt that he had been listening in to another's private conversation when he ought to have simply returned to his bed – but why was Georgina so willing to listen and talk with the doctor but had been so unwilling to have him even sit with her for a short time?

Still confused and a little troubled by this, Gideon found himself unwilling to retire to bed. Instead, he sat by the fire and let his gaze land on the flickering flames, trying to find some peace and comfort in a situation that suddenly seemed to be turning itself on its head, all over again.

CHAPTER SIXTEEN

The next few days passed with an increasing slowness. Georgina declared herself to be still much too weak and tired to even consider traveling to the Dunstable estate and, given that he could not exactly argue with her, Gideon found himself having to do nothing other than wait for the lady. There was no point in returning to the estate and making preparations for her and for their wedding if he had no idea of when she might be willing to attend with him.

On occasion, Gideon would find himself wandering through the streets of London, always finding his feet turning towards Smithfield Market and the church that held the Devil's basement, but for whatever reason, he never went within. Perhaps it was because he did not want to bring himself any additional pain in seeing Josephine, or perhaps it was because he did not know what he would say if he saw her.

His heart was still full of her, no matter what he tried

to do. Georgina, even in her weakness, still grated on him. She was growing increasingly demanding, even though she had her companion and at least two maids to care for her, and only really quietened whenever Doctor Thomas came by to visit – which he had begun to do fairly often. It was as though he could not keep away, although he continued to state to Gideon that he needed to ensure that Miss Wells was not weakening and was, as he hoped, continuing to grow stronger with every day that passed.

Gideon often heard them both talking, for the bedchamber door was always left ajar for propriety's sake, but he found it almost laughable that there should be such considerations when the doctor's visits lasted for hours upon hours. There were fewer and fewer patients at the Devil's basement, from what Gideon understood, and Doctor Thomas found this new patient of his to be something of a refreshment. Apparently talking to Georgina brought the doctor a new lease of life, freeing him from the pain and difficulties he had endured these last weeks. Or so Doctor Thomas had said when Gideon had asked him whether or not something was wrong with Georgina, given that he had spent a long while with her.

The man had flushed and looked away, but it had not prevented him from returning and doing the same all over again. In fact, it seemed that both the doctor and Georgina were eager for these visits to continue, given just how delighted they appeared to be with one another's company. And yet, whenever Gideon went in to speak to Georgina, she did not appear to care much for his conversation or the like. She usually fell fairly silent and did not look at him much, claiming tiredness for her

CHAPTER 16

lack of conversation and often sending him away to fetch her something or other.

A slow hope had begun to burn in Gideon's heart and, whilst he had not questioned Georgina on the subject, he had begun to let himself believe that things might come to a rather satisfactory conclusion after all. He had never really believed that Georgina would allow herself to stoop as low as to marry a doctor but, mayhap if the doctor was given a little encouragement to ask her, then Gideon might find himself in a position where he was free to marry someone entirely different.

"My lord!"

Turning away from the window where he had been musing, Gideon saw the butler hurrying towards him with a note in his hand.

"Thank you." Taking it from him, he turned the letter over and saw that the seal was that of Viscount Armitage, Georgina's father. Now the agitation of the butler became clear. Breaking open the seal, he read the lines swiftly, before smiling at the butler.

"Your master is quite all right," he said, calmly. "He has been ill but has recovered. Apparently, he took ill on the journey home and has been resting at an inn somewhere. You need not fear any longer, my good man. Viscount Armitage is recovering, just as his daughter is."

The butler clasped his hands, joy evident in his face. "Oh, thank you, my lord," he breathed, as though Gideon himself had been the sole reason for Lord Armitage's recovery. "I shall go and inform the rest of the staff at this very moment!"

Gideon chuckled. "Very well." He waited until the

butler had left the room before reading the note again, frowning just a little as he read about just how close the viscount had come to death. He would not allow Georgina to hear of that for fear that it would send her into a deep distress, although he ought to go and inform her at once that her father was both alive and well. It would come as a great relief to her, he was sure.

"Georgina?" he called, as he hurried up the staircase two at a time. "Georgina, I have some excellent news!"

Frowning, he realized that the bedchamber door was firmly shut, which was somewhat unusual. Pausing for a moment, he rapped quietly on the door, a little concerned that he might waken her from her slumber.

"Georgina?" he called, as quietly as he could. "I have some news of your father."

There was a muffled noise from within, which brought Gideon even more concern. "Georgina?" he called again, rapping all the harder. "Are you quite all right?"

"Yes, yes." The door opened to reveal none other than Doctor Thomas, who stepped aside to allow Gideon to enter. "I was just ensuring that Miss Wells was continuing with her improvements."

Something like thunder rattled all through Gideon. He was just about to demand to know why the door was closed and what the doctor had been about by speaking to Georgina in such a private space, only to notice that Georgina's maid was standing in the corner, quietly folding away a few blankets. His anger faded in a moment, feeling himself grow hot with the embarrassment over what he had been about to say.

CHAPTER 16

"And are you improving still, Georgina?" he asked, walking quickly into the room and seeing Georgina sitting quietly in a chair by the fire, fully dressed and looking quite the thing.

"I am," Georgina replied, looking up at him with the faintest hint of pink in her cheeks. "Doctor Thomas thinks I am doing very well."

"I am glad to hear it," Gideon murmured, taking in Georgina's appearance and thinking to himself that yes, she did look a good deal better than before. Her eyes were sparkling, her color was good and, for the first time since she had returned to her townhouse, she appeared to be quite willing to speak to him.

"I have a note from your father, Georgina," he continued, sitting down opposite her. "Should you like to hear the news?"

Georgina leaned forward, her smile fading at once. "Yes, indeed," she said quickly, fear wrapping itself across her face. "Is it bad news? I have been so very worried."

"No," Gideon answered quickly, wanting to keep her fear at bay. "He is quite well."

Doctor Thomas cleared his throat. "I had best excuse myself," he muttered, quietly. "The Devil's basement is to be cleaned top to bottom now that all the patients have left us and I should oversee that. Do excuse me."

Georgina looked up at him, ignoring Gideon completely. "But you will return, will you not?"

Doctor Thomas inclined his head. "Tomorrow, of course. Good day, Miss Wells. Good day, Lord Dunstable."

"Good day," Gideon muttered, not quite sure what to

make of this exchange. The fact that Georgina seemed so keen to have the doctor's company still brought up a good many questions and, as he waited for the doctor to quit the room, Gideon determined that he would ask Georgina about it all.

"My father," Georgina said, bringing him back to what they had been discussing. "How is he?"

Gideon gave her a small smile, trying to reassure her further. "He was ill but he has now recovered," he said, gently. "You need not worry, my dear. He is at his estate now and is trying to regain his strength, much as you are."

"Oh." Georgina put one hand to her mouth, her eyes blinking rapidly as tears pressed against them. She remained so for a moment or two, sitting back in her chair as if to keep Gideon from reaching out to comfort her. "Then I should return home, should I not?"

Gideon shook his head. "No, indeed. I will make sure to inform your father that we are to wed just as soon as you are better. He will travel to the Dunstable estate for the wedding, just as we had thought. We will need to give him a few weeks to recover, however."

Georgina did not appear to be best pleased with this idea, for her brows furrowed and lines of anxiety and concern wrapped themselves across her forehead. She looked away from him towards the fire, her teeth tugging gently at her lip.

"Georgina?" Gideon asked quietly. "Is something the matter?"

She started as though she had not quite heard him, only to stammer something awkward and look away.

Gideon pushed again, a little more firmly this time, determined to discover the source of her displeasure.

"Georgina," he said, her eyes darting to his for only a moment. "There is something troubling you and I wish to know what it is. Speak to me, will you not?"

She shook her head, a mournful sigh leaving her lips.

"You do not wish to wed me, is that it?" Gideon asked, feeling himself stir a little with excitement. "Tell me the truth, Georgina. I will not be angry with you if you do so."

Slowly, so slowly, she turned her head towards him and looked at him steadily. "You will think me terrible, Dunstable," she said, hoarsely, her eyes filled with a sheen of sparkling tears. "A lady does not break off her engagement for a man as unsuitable as –"

Stopping dead, she slammed one hand over her mouth, her eyes wide and staring as she looked back at him as if expecting him to throw himself from the chair in anger.

Everything slowly began to make sense.

"Oh, Georgina," he murmured, quietly. "You need not be fearful of breaking the engagement between us, not if you do not care for me in that way. Our marriage would not be one that would make either of us happy."

She dropped her hand to her lap and stared at him almost stupefied.

"I know," he continued, his lips curved in a small smile. "I have been thinking about our attachment for some time, my dear. I apologize that I have not said anything to you as yet but I could not bring myself to do so, not when you were so dreadfully ill and certainly not when you so evidently needed me."

"I – I can hardly believe this," Georgina breathed, her eyes no longer sparkling with tears but rather slowly filling with delight. "Are you stating, Dunstable, that you do not wish to marry me after all?"

Gideon smiled and leaned forward. "My dear Georgina, I would have married you without a moment of hesitation, given that it was my duty and that I had agreed to the marriage. However, I confess that I do not think that either of us would be particularly happy in such a marriage. Do you?"

"No," she said honestly, flopping back in her chair in apparent relief. "Oh, Dunstable, I was quite content up until the moment I looked up and saw the look in Doctor Thomas' eyes."

One of Gideon's eyebrows shot up. "Doctor Thomas?"

She blushed scarlet. "Do not tease me, Dunstable. Surely you must have surmised that it was not exactly my health that has kept him here so long these last few days.

Gideon drew in a long breath, sat back in his chair and let out a long sigh. "I will admit to you, Georgina, I was not quite sure what to make of it all. I am glad, however, that you have been able to speak honestly to me about this matter."

Georgina looked at him and, for the first time, Gideon felt as though she were being completely open and honest with him. There was a vulnerability in her gaze that brought a warmth to his heart, glad that she was finally able to speak to him with such honesty.

CHAPTER 16

"Dunstable," she said, softly. "Doctor Thomas wants to marry me."

The smile faded from his face, not because he thought it a terrible notion but rather because he knew what such a marriage would mean.

"He is not a titled gentleman, Georgina," he said, slowly. "He is a working man. He has a practice, patients, and all sorts of responsibilities. It would mean a very big change for someone such as you."

Georgina nodded, her expression growing thoughtful. "And yet I find that I would not dislike such a change," she said, slowly. "In fact, I feel as though the life I could have with Doctor Thomas would be worth all the difficulties in the world."

There was a moment of silence, a moment where Gideon himself reflected on what changes would come to his own life, now that he was free to ask Josephine to marry him. For her, in particular, it would mean a very different way of living and he would have to ensure that he cared nothing for what others would think of their difference in station. But for Georgina to consider marrying Doctor Thomas was another thing entirely. She would have no title, although Gideon was quite sure her father, Lord Armitage, would ensure that they had a respectable home with a good many servants if she were to marry someone as lowly as the doctor.

"Your father will not be pleased, Georgina," he finished, trying to ensure that she had taken everything into account. "What will he say to the news of your intention to wed a doctor?"

Georgina smiled, her eyes bright. "He will not know

until he can do nothing to change it," she replied, her smile a little teasing. "Not unless you tell him, of course."

"You intend to elope?" Gideon asked, flabbergasted. "Truly?"

"Truly," Georgina replied, with a slight shrug of her shoulders. "Why ever not? That way, my father cannot object and drag me away somewhere until I supposedly come to my senses!"

Gideon had to admit that this was, perhaps, a welcome consideration. "He may cut you off."

"Then I shall learn how to be a doctor's wife and nothing more," Georgina answered, with a good deal of firmness. "But I do not think it will come to that, do you? My father dotes on me, given that I am his only daughter, and whilst he may refuse to speak or see me for a time, I am quite sure that, come the end of it, he will be happy to see me eventually. You need not worry for me, Gideon. I will be quite all right."

Gideon let out a long, slow breath, trying to make sense of all that had been said. "I am to leave you here in London, alone, without informing your father?"

A sudden giggle escaped from Georgina. "I am not as weak as I appear, Dunstable. I have been doing it a little too brown of late, simply to try and ascertain Doctor Thomas' intentions before I made my decision. Once you are gone from London, I intend to leave with Doctor Thomas almost at once. He is not exactly poor, you know. He can hire a carriage and the like so that we can make our journey to Scotland almost at once. Then, we shall return here."

CHAPTER 16

Gideon's eyebrows shot into his hair. "Here? Into your father's townhouse?"

Georgina giggled again. "Indeed. Why would I not? It is much more suitable than the dingy little house Doctor Thomas has described. Besides, my father does not exactly use his house very often. Only once a year and only for a few weeks at that! No, I am quite sure that it will all work out splendidly, Dunstable."

This pretty little speech sent Gideon into a myriad of confusing thoughts. Part of him wanted to stay and lecture Georgina that she ought to think a good deal more carefully about this before she went to marry Doctor Thomas, particularly as regarded her father, whereas the other part of him said that he simply should leave well alone. After all, he had done his duty for Georgina, had he not? He had cared for her, ensured that she was well taken care of and now that she was restored to full health, his responsibilities had come to an end, particularly if she did not wish for him to care for her any longer!

"Go."

He looked up to see Georgina smiling at him. Her face was bright, her expression one of sheer delight and he found himself smiling back at her, thinking that he had never seen her so happy before. It was quite clear that Doctor Thomas was the one who had brought such a change about and, for that, he was rather thankful.

"Go!" Georgina said again, laughing. "Doctor Thomas is just outside, waiting to see what my decision has been and, should you still be here, then I cannot exactly try to elope now, can I?"

Shaking his head for a moment in an attempt to

understand all that had just taken place, Gideon got to his feet and looked down at Georgina, feeling his heart slowly begin to quicken with a wonderful anticipation. He could go to Josephine now and profess his love for her without being held back by duty or expectation. Somehow, he had been given his freedom.

"You will write to your father?" he asked, seeing Georgina nod. "I would not like him to be waiting anxiously to hear you are safe. You know how he cares for you."

"I do," Georgina said, promising to do so. "And thank you, Dunstable, for all you have done. I am sorry things have not worked out as we had intended."

Gideon chuckled, taking Georgina's hand and bowing over it. "You need not apologize, my dear," he replied, with a smile. "In fact, it is I who ought to be thanking you. I shall go now and leave you with your husband to be. May I offer you my congratulations, my dear."

She smiled at him. "Thank you, Dunstable."

Hurrying towards the bedchamber door, he opened it to find Doctor Thomas looking at him in a somewhat guilty fashion.

"Doctor Thomas," Gideon smiled, his expression bright. "Do come in. Let me shake your hand firmly and be the first to wish you happy."

Doctor Thomas' expression was first astonished, and then delighted. He strode across to Gideon and shook his hand firmly, his eyes a little wide as though he expected Gideon to plant him a facer without any provocation.

"All is well," Gideon promised, quietly. "Treat her with all kindness, Doctor Thomas."

"I will," Doctor Thomas replied, fervently. "Thank you, Lord Dunstable. You do not know what this means to me."

Gideon chuckled. "Nor do you know what it means to me, Doctor Thomas. If you will excuse me, I must go to the Devil's basement. I have a young lady to find."

He did not stop to tell the wide-eyed doctor that, yes, it was Josephine to whom he referred, for the urgency in his heart pushed him all the harder to leave the house at once. Neither did Gideon hear the squeal of delight from Georgina as Doctor Thomas hurried into the room to wrap her in his arms. All of his thoughts, all of his intent, was focused solely on reaching Josephine and confessing his love to her, in the hope she would agree to become his wife. He could think of no-one better.

All she had to do was say yes.

CHAPTER SEVENTEEN

Josephine swept the floor for what felt like the hundredth time, her back and shoulders aching from the work she had done today. The basement was now cleared of patients and for that, she was more than glad. The fever seemed to have lifted from London town. Slowly, carefully, it had let go its grip of death on the London streets. The basement had been scrubbed, washed and scrubbed again, in an effort to remove the stench of disease and death that had lingered in it for so long.

"I'd best be going."

She turned her head to see Sam standing at the bottom of the stairs, looking a good deal happier than she had ever seen him. His eyes were bright, his clothes as neat as they could be and the smile on his face lifted her heart all the more.

"Sam," she said, quietly. "Are you to go to the Dunstable estate?"

He nodded. "I got word that the first carriage is leaving this afternoon," he said, quietly, although Josephine could sense the excitement within him. "I do not know if Miss Wells is to continue after, although I would expect so."

Josephine nodded, turning her head so that Sam would not see the pain on her face. Every time she thought of Lord Dunstable, every time she thought of his marriage to Miss Wells, she felt the same stab of pain that almost left her breathless.

"I'll miss speaking to you, Josephine," Sam said, coming over to embrace her. "We've worked hard these last few weeks. We've taken on death together."

"And sometimes, we triumphed," Josephine replied, hugging him tightly. "But you're to have a place of your own now, Sam. Lord Dunstable will take good care of you."

He puffed out his chest as he stepped back, his limp barely noticeable. "I'm to work in the stables, with the horses."

Josephine smiled, truly glad for her friend. "And do you like horses?"

He chuckled. "I'm going to have to! But all the same, Josephine, I'm thankful for what you did in getting me a place of my own."

A sudden idea took a hold of Josephine and, asking Sam to wait for a moment, she rushed to where she kept her few belongings. Raking through them quickly, she found what she was looking for in a moment, clasping the bundle tightly in her hand as she hurried back to Sam.

"Here," she said, handing the package to him. "You're

to take this. It's just the beginning of your savings, for when it's time to put your feet up and rest."

He stared at her for a moment, before slowly unwrapping the cloth. Gasping in astonishment, his eyes widened as he stared at the coins, given to her so long ago by Lord Dunstable.

"Josephine, I can't take these!" he exclaimed, trying to hand them back to her. "You'll need them."

"No," she replied, pushing his hand away gently. "I won't. I have a place with Doctor Thomas now. He'll take care of me." She did not mention that keeping the coins would only make her pine for Lord Dunstable, did not murmur that they would only bring her painful memories all over again. Instead, she repeatedly insisted that Sam take them for himself, until he had no other choice but to hesitantly accept.

His eyes filled and Josephine embraced him again, glad that she could do something to help her friend. Yes, he had a position with Lord Dunstable, but in time, he would need to find a place of his own to live out the last years, and she wanted him to be comfortable.

"An angel," Sam said, pressing her hand tightly with his. "That is what you are, Miss Josephine. An angel."

She smiled at him and kissed his cheek, surprised at the amount of pain she felt over their parting. Sam was like family to her, she realized. A good friend and a good man, who had shown her so much in his dedication and good character. Goodness, she was going to miss him.

"I'll try and get someone to write to you," Sam said, moving away from Josephine and back towards the basement steps. "I can't write much but I'm sure there'll be someone there who can help me."

"I'd like that," Josephine replied, in a voice that cracked with emotion. "Goodbye, Sam."

He nodded, smiled and climbed the staircase, leaving her alone in the basement. Josephine tried not to cry, tried not to let the tears come into her eyes and yet the pain of parting, of being left all alone once again, bit hard at her. Wiping her eyes with the back of her hand, she picked up her broom and resumed sweeping, telling herself that this was the last difficult hurdle she was to face. Tomorrow, when the Devil's basement was finally closed for good, she would have a new life with Doctor Thomas. She had already seen the small but cozy room that would be her own. It had everything she would need and it had brought her a measure of happiness. It would never ease the ache and the pain that came with having to leave Lord Dunstable behind.

"This place looks remarkably different."

She froze in place, closing her eyes tightly It could not be him, she told herself, her hands tightening on the broom. It could not be Lord Dunstable. He was making preparations to return to his estate, so why would he return here?

"When I first saw it," he continued, making Josephine's stomach clench. "It was not as it is now. It was so full of pain and grief that I could hardly bear it. But look at it now."

Her breath came in short, sharp gasps as she turned around to see Lord Dunstable standing before her with a small smile playing about his lips. The light of the lanterns lit up his features, sending fire into his eyes, and Josephine felt herself unable to look away.

"I could not leave London without you," he said tenderly, moving a little closer to her. "I could not do it, Josephine."

"Please." She held up one hand to him, stopping him from coming any closer. "Please, do not, Lord Dunstable. I cannot bear it."

Thankfully, he remained where he was. "I could not bear it either, Josephine," he replied, his voice echoing around the room and surrounding her entirely. "I could not bear to be parted from you and yet, when it came to Georgina and her illness, I knew that I had to be true to my obligations."

She nodded, her eyes burning with unshed tears. "I am aware of it all, Lord Dunstable. I have never blamed you for stepping away. It was foolish of me not to realize sooner that what you said to me came from your delirium."

A dark frown pulled his brow low. "What do you mean?" he asked, taking a step closer to her. "My delirium? What is it that you are talking about?"

Swallowing the lump in her throat, Josephine set the broom aside, feeling the old familiar pain slicing through her again. "When you told me that you cared for me at the lake," she whispered, her voice refusing to give any weight to her words. "You had the fever then. To then confess that you – that you...." She trailed off, unable to say those deeply personal words.

"When I told you that I loved you," Lord Dunstable finished, gently, looking tenderly at her. "Is that what you were to say?"

Nodding, Josephine dragged in a painful breath, wanting to ask him why he was forcing her to endure this all again. "I knew then that I was mistaken," she continued, letting the truth drag out of her. "You were lost in your fever, speaking words you did not know. You must have thought that I was Miss Wells."

A sudden laugh had her looking up, her eyes widening with astonishment at the mirth in his expression. She did not know what to make of it, standing there in the basement alone with Lord Dunstable.

"My dear lady," Lord Dunstable chuckled, shaking his head. "I have never cared for Miss Wells and I have certainly never loved her. Whatever gave you that impression?"

Stammering, she tried to explain, her heart slamming wildly in her chest as she tried to think about what this might mean. "When you came to see her," she breathed, one hand over her pounding heart as if to silence it. "I saw the expression on your face."

He shook his head. "The love you saw there, Josephine, that was for you."

Unable to believe what she had just heard, Josephine put one hand over her mouth, stumbling backwards as weakness ran through her. Lord Dunstable caught her at once, holding her tightly against him as she stared up into his eyes, hardly daring to believe that it was true.

"But what about Miss Wells?" she asked, unable to

move forward into his embrace without knowing what had become of his fiancée. "What of your obligations to her?"

He lifted one shoulder, a broad smile on his face. "They are no longer required, Josephine. Georgina has decided that she cares for Doctor Thomas more than I."

"Doctor Thomas?" she breathed, her astonishment growing with every moment. "Do you mean that they - ?"

"They are to wed," he answered, his smile spreading all the more. "They are to elope this evening, if they have not left already. I am quite free, Josephine. I am no longer bound by my obligations."

"Free?" The word left her mouth in a whisper, feeling his arms encase her tightly. This was the moment she had never believed would come to pass and yet, as she looked at him, she saw in his eyes that it was true.

"My dear Josephine," he whispered, tenderly. "I have stayed with Georgina simply because I had to. I could not turn from her when she was in such desperate need of my aid. Her father was ill – although he is recovering now – and she had no-one else to turn to. I am a gentleman of honor and I swore I would do my duty and honor the agreement I had made with her, despite the broken heart that I would carry with me for the rest of my days."

She blinked furiously, pushing away the tears that had sprang into her eyes. "Broken heart?" she repeated, wondering if he had been enduring the same anguished torment as she.

His fingers brushed lightly down her cheek. "Yes, Josephine. My heart has been breaking over and over in the knowledge that I would never be able to call you my own. I had intended to come to London to break off my engagement with Georgina, so that I might propose to you, but the fever changed everything. Now, however, I can finally do what I have longed for."

Her breathing was so rapid that she thought she might faint, made all the more profound by the fact that Lord Dunstable lowered his head and caught her lips with his.

It was as if she were in a dream. She could do nothing more than cling to him, her arms tight about his neck as he held her tightly around the waist. His kiss was warm and sweet, bringing her to such exaltations that she thought she might laugh and cry and scream all at once.

"There," he breathed, his lips only a little away from her own. "There, you see, Josephine? I *do* care for you, most ardently. I love you."

Resting her head against his chest for a moment, Josephine closed her eyes and drew in her breath again and again, trying to calm her frantically beating heart. This was real. This was not a dream that she was to wake up from. Lord Dunstable was here, holding her in his arms and offering her his heart.

"I have loved you for many days," she whispered, unable to raise her head. "But I never imagined that such a thing as this would ever truly occur. I am nothing more than an orphaned girl, alone in the world and you –"

"You are the most perfect, the most wonderful, the most delightful lady I have ever known," he interrupted, gently. "I want you to be my wife, Josephine. I want you to be my baroness and come to live with me in my estate, forever. I want you to make my home your home, to live with me in love and tenderness. Say that you will, my love. Say that you will be my bride."

"I know nothing of being a baroness," Josephine exclaimed, suddenly afraid. "What if I do not please your mother or your sister?"

Lord Dunstable shook his head. "They will love you just as much as I. Francine herself encouraged me in this, my love." His eyes grew gentle as he cupped her face in his hands. "And you will be the most wonderful baroness, Josephine. For your kind heart, your generous nature and your sweetness of temper will endear everyone to you. They will all love you, just as I have come to love you."

Josephine looked up at Lord Dunstable and felt her heart overflow. She could not refuse him now, not when he was so earnest. "Oh, Dunstable," she whispered, feeling as though finally, she was to have all that she had ever dreamed of. "I love you desperately. Yes, I will marry you."

He closed his eyes for a moment, caught up in his joy. She leaned into him, holding him tightly, finally at peace. She would not be alone any longer, she would no longer be without a home. Her love for Lord Dunstable was returned, bringing her more happiness and joy than she had ever imagined.

"Come then, my love," Lord Dunstable whispered in her ear, his lips trailing across her cheek. "Let me take you home."

"Home," she whispered, looking up at him with sparkling eyes. "Home with you, my love."

"Where you will always stay," he replied, lowering his head a little more. "Living together in love, for today and always."

MY DEAR READER

Thank you for reading and supporting my books! I hope this story brought you some escape from the real world into the always captivating Regency world. A good story, especially one with a happy ending, just brightens your day and makes you feel good! If you enjoyed the book, would you leave a review on Amazon? Reviews are always appreciated.

Below is a complete list of all my books! Why not look for them on Amazon and see if one of them can keep you entertained for a few hours?

The Duke's Daughters Series
The Duke's Daughters: A Sweet Regency Romance Boxset

A Rogue for a Lady
My Restless Earl
Rescued by an Earl
In the Arms of an Earl
The Reluctant Marquess (Prequel)

A Smithfield Market Regency Romance
The Smithfield Market Romances: A Sweet Regency Romance Boxset

A Rogue's Flower
Saved by the Scoundrel
Mending the Duke
The Baron's Malady

Love and Christmas Wishes: Three Regency Romance Novellas

Happy Reading!

All my love,

Rose

Printed in Great Britain
by Amazon